Desperate Lies

Ella Miles

EllaMiles.com

Ella@ellamiles.com

LIES SERIES

Lies We Share: A Prologue

Vicious Lies
Desperate Lies
Fated Lies
Cruel Lies
Dangerous Lies
Endless Lies

PROLOGUE
LIESEL

I WANT TO KILL LANGSTON, but I'd also die for him.

He ruined my life.

He made me so desperate to get my life back that I'm about to murder in cold blood.

Langston took every-fucking-thing from me.

He took my money.

My career.

My heart.

My soul.

My life.

He took the one person I care about above all.

Langston couldn't just be happy taking me, controlling me, demanding I give up my life to pay for my sins—he wanted more.

And he won't stop until he has everything.

I'm pretty sure he already does.

But at least I'll take the one thing from him he truly loves. I'm desperate to find out the truth, to find out if he really took everything. This is the only way to separate the truth from the lies.

I've always been the huntress, but I'm about to become the killer...

1
LIESEL

I LIED—THOSE words flood me as I run down the beach.

Should I run on the sand where it's easier to run, but I'm an open target? Or should I dart into the jungle where I'll have to fight through thick brush, but I won't be spotted?

I decide speed is better than cover and keep running down the beach, away from Langston's house, and toward the airport.

I lied.

I'm not really married to Waylon.

Langston lied, too, right?

We lie—that's what we do. All we've done is lie to each other since we were kids. That's what we were doing—lying. Not letting the other person see our cards.

He definitely lied. There is no way Langston is married to my cousin, Phoenix, and already has two kids. Siren or Kai would have said something to me.

Right?

RIGHT?

Yes.

Langston is just as single as ever.

He may be dating Phoenix, hedging his bets so if I don't marry him, he can still marry a Dunn and go after my inheritance.

Boom.

I duck at the sound, covering my head like somehow my hands are going to be able to stop a bomb.

I shield my eyes as I glance up at the sun, trying to see if we are being attacked from above. I don't see any planes.

It's a ground attack; probably someone who wants Enzo and Kai's empire like usual. There is a reason I don't really hang out with them anymore—this is why. I'd rather not be ambushed and spend my time running from guns, bombs, and dangerous people every second of every day.

I prefer to be able to go to an excluded beach island to actually relax and not worry about bombs being dropped on my head—call me high-maintenance.

I hear gunfire behind me.

Jesus.

How did I end up in this world? When will it end?

I decide that I should take the jungle route after all. I slip between some bushes, scratching my arms and causing some nasty red bumps to pop up.

Another loud bomb goes off.

I stop and turn my head in the direction of the house.

"You better not destroy the house!" I yell into the jungle. I plan on taking the house from Langston someday. I may not like Langston anymore, but I dreamt up that fucking house when I was eight—it's mine.

I turn back in the opposite direction of the house, hoping to eventually find the runway we landed on.

I take a step, and a green leaf with tiny razor-sharp teeth digs into my thigh. I take another step and almost trip over a branch. One more step, and then I stop.

There is no clear path. I realize now that when I followed Langston to the house, he was clearing the path for me, stomping down leaves and branches. He was making it easier for me, even if he was teasing me by letting his branches hit me.

Now, I'm all alone to make my own path. I like being an independent woman carving my own path.

I sigh, covered in sweat dripping down my forehead and pooling around the base of my neck. Getting off this island is going to take forever.

I curse to hell whoever it is attacking. I'd rather be stuck talking to Langston than running for my life through the hot jungle.

Why am I running?

Does Langston think I'm not strong enough to stay and fight with him?

Will he be too worried about me if I'm nearby while he's fighting?

Or is he hiding something?

My money is on Langston hiding something. He doesn't want me to know who's attacking. Or he doesn't want them to know that I'm here.

Either way, he's hiding.

That alone should make me turn my ass around and demand answers from Langston.

My leg is straddling a fallen tree; my hair is stuck to my face. I would do anything for some water to fix my bone-dry mouth, too.

I look left then right.

What do I do?

Do I run back to Langston, into the danger, and demand answers?

Do I do as Langston said and run? And run? And run?

I'm already running; I'm not turning back now.

He said to run as far as I could tonight, and then to come find him tomorrow.

He's crazy if he thinks I'll return to him—back to being his captive and back to the place where he said he'd end my life.

There is no way I'm going back now.

Langston promised me answers. He promised to give me one clue from his half of the torn paper.

I look left—toward Langston—man, do I want to know what his half of the paper says. I want to know what my dad's last message to me was. I want to know because I'm curious—not because I give a damn about the treasure.

I make my own money—I don't need any inheritance or treasure.

I may have had some help from Enzo, giving me enough money to go to college and feed myself, but after college I got a job. I worked hard. I've even offered many times to pay Enzo back. He just never accepts my money.

Good riddance, I huff, pulling myself over the log.

A mistake—I come crashing down into a pile of mud on the other side.

Can this day get any worse?

My shoulder throbs, reminding me of my bullet wound. Memories flash, reminding me of the rape, the abuse, the child I gave up.

Yes, this day can get a lot worse.

I sit up as I hear more gunfire.

Langston said to run.

No one can move very quickly through this thick brush, but I should start moving faster in case anyone starts following me—mainly Langston.

So I force myself to get up.

I force my legs to run.

And run, and run, and run.

I stop thinking about Langston.

I stop wondering and analyzing his words—trying to determine if he lied or not.

I stop worrying that a stray bullet or misplaced bomb is going to blow me into a million tiny pieces.

I focus on putting one step in front of the other.

Again.

And again.

And again.

Until the sun has set.

Until it's pitch-black outside.

And even then I keep going.

I refuse to be killed.

I refuse to be anyone's captive.

I refuse to let any man control me.

I take another step.

This step makes all the difference.

I may not be able to see very well, but I don't hear the crunch of leaves. I don't have to dodge low hanging limbs. I don't feel the brush of branches scratching my mud and sweat covered skin.

My feet sink into sand.

Did I take a wrong step toward the beach instead of walking in a straight line to the airport?

Or did I make it?

I take another and another.

The concrete of the runway greets my feet.

I smile for the first time all day. I bite my bottom lip as the grin spreads.

My lip—Langston's kiss.

No, stop thinking about him, brain.

Focus.

I made it to the runway. There are no airplanes stored here, but I've spotted a handful of planes landing on this island while I've spent my time here. There are planes that fly here that don't belong to Langston Pearce.

There will be a plane if I wait here long enough for one to land.

Tomorrow, come find me, huntress.

Langston's words ring in my ear.

I don't have time to wait—to get lucky.

I make my own luck.

There is a small building near the runway. It looks more like an outhouse than an actual building, but I have to try something.

When I get to the entrance, I realize there isn't even a door.

I exhale loudly.

I'm not counting on there being anyone inside, or any electronics to call for help.

I step inside anyway.

The room is dark. I search the wall with my hand, but I don't find a light switch.

I should just leave, but it's the middle of the night.

The explosions and gunfire stopped—not that that's comforting. It means Langston is probably looking for me now. If I head into the jungle again, I have to deal with jaguars, venomous snakes, poisonous spiders.

I need sleep if I'm going to have any energy to face tomorrow. This tiny building is better than sleeping on the jungle floor.

There isn't a door, but there are at least three walls to protect me.

I lie down on the floor and curl up in a ball as I hear rain starting overhead.

Please, let the roof be waterproof.

I cross my fingers, squinting my eyes up at the dark roof.

After five minutes pass and I'm not wet, I realize my luck might have changed. At least the roof is holding.

A soft smile spreads as I close my eyes and begin to drift off to sleep from exhaustion with the help of the lightly tapping rain. The rain will make it harder for Langston to find me. And he won't think I made it all the way to the runway in one night.

Tonight, I'll sleep soundly. Tomorrow…

A buzzing wakes me up.

I blink rapidly, trying to make sense of my surroundings. I've been sleeping in a closet, and this room isn't much bigger than that, but it's not Langston's closet.

I moan, wishing a buzzing noise would stop and let me sleep. It's still dark outside. I have no idea how long I've been asleep, but it can't be more than a couple of hours at best.

More buzzing.

Wait—buzzing!

There is something electronic in this room. It's probably just a battery-powered alarm clock, but I can hope.

I move onto all fours as I pat around the floor, searching for the source of the buzzing.

I feel a strap.

A bag!

It's sitting on a small chair in the corner.

I pick up the bag and put it on my lap, as I furiously search inside.

My heart races. *Could I really find a phone? A way to make contact with the outside world and escape?*

I touch a piece of glass.

My heart thumps to a stop.

It's too big to be a phone.

I pull out the device—an iPad.

My heart flutters, not knowing if I should be elated or crushed.

I click the home button to get the screen to light up—praying that the iPad has a cellular connection. I doubt there is wifi.

Please, please, please.

I stare at the screen after the split second it takes to light up. I silence the alarm buzzing the device.

My eyes dart to the upper right corner.

It has cellular reception.

Thank god.

I pull up the phone app and am about to call Waylon when my fingers suddenly stop.

I don't know what island I'm on. I care about Waylon. He's a smart man, but he's never had to worry about money, never gotten scrappy or creative, never dealt with dangerous people. The most he'll be able to do is call the police or FBI to search for me.

By then, Langston will have found me and moved me to another island.

But who else do I have on my side?

Enzo?

No, he'd take Langston's side.

Kai?

She's sweet, but becoming a leader has made her tougher. She will do whatever is in the best interest of the empire she controls, which means not pissing off one of her best employees—Langston. She would help me and then rat me out to him.

Zeke?

He's always hated me. He wouldn't help.

Siren...?

Siren! She's my answer. Yes, she and Langston have a weird relationship that I will never understand. They say they are just friends, but I've always wondered if Zeke and Siren have an open relationship. There is no way she and Langston got so close without fucking each other's brains out.

That might seem to make her the last person on earth I should call to help me, but because Siren is so close to Langston, she will call him out on his bullshit. There is no way any of them: Enzo, Kai, Zeke, or Siren would be okay with Langston kidnapping me and threatening to kill me.

But three out of the four will stand by Langston because he's one of them. Sure, they've been nice to me over the years, but I've never been one of them—not truly.

Siren is the only one who will put a stop to this.

I dial Siren's number from memory. Most people in this day and age don't have many numbers memorized. Call it a skill I learned from being poor, but you never know when you are going to not have a phone, or when you're going to be in a dangerous situation and need someone's help.

Like right now.

I don't expect Siren to answer—I'm calling from an unknown number. And it's the middle of the night, or at least, it's the middle of the night in whatever time zone I'm in.

"Hello?" Siren answers on the second ring.

I let out a long, steadying breath, putting all of my trust into this woman.

"I need your help."

2
LANGSTON

I WATCH Liesel run away from me.

Somehow, I keep my feet firmly planted in the sand.

I try to ignore all of her features—her toned legs, tight ass, feminine curve of her hips, long untamed hair. It's like all of her features were specially designed just for me. She's my ultimate temptation; one I will never succumb to.

I kissed her to wake her up from her nightmare. That's it. That's all that kiss was. It wasn't weakness. It wasn't losing control. It wasn't a slip.

At least that's what I keep telling myself.

Liesel keeps running down the beach, around the edge of the island, until the jungle brush blocks my view. I don't know if she stays on the beach or bolts into the forest. She's gone, and I have no idea if she's coming back.

My throat dries, turning into ash at that thought. She has to come back. I don't have all the information I need from her.

Married.

That's what she said. She's married to that old fucker.

Liesel just said that because of what was on her half of

the letter. I suspected that marriage was the first step in searching for Liesel's inheritance based on what my half of the letter said.

But Liesel married—it doesn't make sense to me. She would never get married just to go after some treasure, and I don't think the woman is capable of falling in love.

No, there is no way Liesel Dunn is married.

My skin begins to boil in jealousy just thinking about Waylon touching her. Proposing to her. Her saying yes. Planning a wedding. Saying I do. And then fucking as husband and wife.

I'm lying to myself. It was all too easy to imagine her married.

I hear gunshots, and I know I can't focus on Liesel anymore. She's safe. No one knows she's here. It's for the best until I can figure out who's attacking us and why.

If Liesel were here, I wouldn't be able to focus. And if she's the target, then she really can't be here. She'd do something stupid like get herself kidnapped.

I don't have my gun on me, which is idiotic. But having a gun on me around Liesel is dangerous—for both of us.

If she smacks off, I might kill her. And if she tricked me and I let my guard down for a single second, she'd find it and kill me. I figured it was for the best to not put either of us in that situation.

I run up the hillside, staying as low as I can to avoid any stray bullets. Our assailants don't seem to have made it past the front of the house. At least my security measures are working.

I make it to the open glass door at the back of the house and peer inside. My team of about a dozen is assembled in the middle of the living room.

I step inside.

"What are you doing standing around? Get to your positions, now!"

"Yes, sir," they all mumble at different times and take off.

I sigh. I really should have found a better number two to train and prepare them for these scenarios better. Especially since I've been spending too much of my free time with Liesel.

Phoenix looks at me with concern in her eyes. "Liesel?"

"She's safe."

She nods.

"I need you to go to the bunker."

"But I can help! I know how to shoot a gun as well as half of these yahoos."

"I know, but you are way more important to me than those yahoos. I pay them to protect us. Your job is to stay safe."

"What about you? Are you going to hide out in the bunker with me?"

I crack my neck back and forth, my face morphing into one of terror, preparing myself for what I'm about to face.

"Don't worry about me, Dunn. No one can touch me if they can't find me."

She frowns. "You're not invincible. You know that, right, Langston?"

I narrow my eyes and grab her hips, pulling her tightly against my body. "I've let these bastards get a ten-minute head start, and they haven't so much as broken the exterior perimeter. Have a little faith in me."

"I do, but I just worry."

I kiss her forehead. "Don't. Go to the bunker. I'll come to you soon."

I step away from her, putting an arm's length of space between us. "Go."

I don't have time to make sure Phoenix gets to the

bunker. She'll either listen to me or she won't. If she doesn't, she'll have to deal with the consequences.

I start to walk away, but Phoenix grabs my hand at the last moment.

"Dunn, I really don't have time—"

She yanks my arm as hard as she can, closing the space between us. Her hands come up to my cheeks, grabbing me hard. She plants a hard, wet, all-out kiss on my lips.

I kiss her back, savoring how her tongue feels in my mouth.

Liesel.

Of course, my dumb-ass brain thinks of my kiss with Liesel instead of enjoying this moment.

When Phoenix kissed me earlier, it was greatly appreciated. I needed something to distract me from my kiss with Liesel. But this kiss now—all it makes me think about is Liesel. She's the last person I want to be thinking about right now.

I want to end the kiss. I need to deal with whatever jackasses are trying to kill us all right now. But if I stop the kiss early, it will only make her desperate to kiss me more.

So I let Phoenix end the kiss.

"Get your ass to the bunker, now. I don't want to have to worry about your safety."

She touches her swollen lip with her finger. She's going to spend her entire time in the bunker thinking about our kiss.

"Dunn," I warn.

"I'm as safe as you are standing here, but fine, I'll go."

I watch as Phoenix walks away toward the more secure half of the house that sits on top of a bunker.

I stare at her legs tightly covered in jeans. I watch the sway of her hips as she walks away. My eyes drift up to her black long-sleeved T-shirt and her short red hair. Phoenix is the complete opposite of Liesel.

I like Phoenix's body, but I don't crave it like an addict craves heroin. With Liesel, if I get the tiniest taste, I'm going to lose myself. I'm going to become so addicted that I won't be able to do anything but think about her.

A loud explosion grabs my attention again.

Jesus, I barely even kissed Liesel, and I'm already going down the rabbit hole. What would happen to me if I did more than kiss her?

That's just one of the many reasons why I can't.

I grab one of my many stashed guns by pressing my finger to the scanner under the kitchen counter. A compartment opens, and I grab the two guns inside, along with plenty of ammunition. Then I take off toward the garage.

The garage is dark when I get there. No one has entered yet.

I run to the Range Rover, pop the door open and then climb in.

This car is bulletproof, and the large tablet inside is hooked up to my entire security system. I'm a great fighter, but the best place for me to help my team is here, being their eyes in the field. My first task is finding the man who ordered this attack so I can put an end to this and save as many lives on my side as possible.

All of his team will end up dead, no matter how many surrender.

I turn on my radio, instantly connecting my voice to my team. "They are only attacking from the front. They're trying to get past the minefield."

"They won't get past it, boss," Seth says.

"Don't get cocky. Be prepared and alert. I'll let you know if any of them get through the perimeter."

I need to find their leader and figure out why they are

attacking. Whoever it is, they aren't very skilled. Or at least, they didn't bring very many men.

I dial Enzo's number. Kai is technically in charge, and I love her to death, but Enzo and I go back since forever. And I don't like to bother Kai and unless it's important.

"What do you need?" Enzo says matter of factly, knowing that I never call him just to chat about how our lives are. I only call when I need something from him.

"The island is under attack. I don't know who it is or if they're after you or me." I leave out the chance that they're attacking to get to Liesel.

"I'm not aware of any threats against us, but let me do a security check and speak with Kai. I'll get back to you in one." He ends the call.

Enzo will call me back in literally one minute. Moments like this are all about speed. I need to know who, where, when, why, and I need to know it all right now.

I zoom in on the men shooting at us. There is nothing special about their clothes, their equipment, nothing that tells me who they work for.

My phone buzzes.

"And?" I answer.

"We don't think they're after us. I'll keep finding out any info I can and leave a message for you. Do you need back-up?" Enzo says with a bit of teasing in his voice. He knows I'm more than capable of handling this myself, and it would take him hours to get here. Even if I did need his help, we'd all be dead by then.

Unfortunately, these men are most likely after us because of Liesel's money. Any leak of a treasure and it brings out all sorts of crazies to try and find it. I don't know how anyone knows when we have taken zero steps to go after the inheritance, but that's a question for a different day.

"Nope, I'm good, brother." I end the call and then look

back at the screen. It's going to take these guys hours to get through the perimeter. I don't have hours. I want this over with now.

Then I can go back to Phoenix and show her I'm still alive.

Then I can go hunt Liesel.

I cock my gun and climb out of the car, ready to put an end to this bullshit they call an attack.

I walk down my driveway.

"What are you doing, boss?" Seth says.

"Ending this. Everyone, hold your positions. Don't interfere unless I tell you to."

I click a button on my phone that stops the minefield from going off so I can meet the men head-on. As I scan the area, I realize they didn't even bring any heavy artillery. The only bombs going off are our own.

I aim my gun through the haze and shoot five men dead.

Then I step through the fog.

I'm an easy target. Any one of the remaining seven men could kill me, but I need a moment to look them all in the eyes to figure out who is most likely to rat out their boss. That man gets to live.

I only need a second to scan. They are all terrified. Any one of them would spill the truth.

I roll my eyes.

Why do men try to attack me like this?

They are so unprepared there is no way they are going to be able to defeat me. It's like they don't care about their men at all.

I don't have a choice but to kill them all. There is no way I'll let any of these men hurt my team or the others I'm protecting. Plus, I don't really need any of them alive to find answers.

Almost bored, I shoot them all one by one. A few get a

couple of bullets off, but the closest to hitting me barely grazes my arm. It's not even close enough to break skin, just to rip my T-shirt.

"Did I miss anyone?" I ask to my team.

"You got them all, boss," Seth answers. Apparently, he's the only one brave enough to answer me after what I did to Joel and Amelia.

I walk over to the closest dead combatant and dig through his clothes until I find his wallet and phone.

"Get to work cleaning up this mess," I tell my team as I take the wallet and phone back to the house.

I pull my earpiece out and pocket my gun, now that the danger has been squashed.

I consider letting Phoenix know that it's safe to come out. *Do I really know it's safe until I find out who's behind the attack and deal with them?*

Plus, I really want to be alone right now.

I run up the stairs, taking them two at a time.

I head to my dresser and find the finger scanner below the top drawer, revealing another hidden gun and a laptop.

I pull out the laptop and bring it to my bed, ignoring the images of Liesel that flash in my head like perfect snapshots.

Stitching up her shoulder.

Holding her in bed.

Her tied up.

I shake my head like a magic eight ball, like I can just shake away my thoughts.

I start typing the name on the driver's license into the computer while I scroll through the phone, finding his most called numbers.

The first number is labeled 'Mom,' so I ignore it.

But the second number has no name associated with it.

This is going to be too easy. I really could use a challenge someday. Maybe that's half the reason I decided to go after Liesel's inheritance.

My head falls back in frustration against the headboard.

I only wish I were just looking for a challenge, and that's why I need Liesel's money. Then I could step away whenever I wanted.

I take a deep breath and then open my eyes. The top search of Edgar Jacobs lists him as a car salesman. Clearly, he's not. It's a front. Just like the bars Enzo and Kai own are fronts for their business. Places that look like normal businesses, but are really the offices of a criminal organization if you look closely.

I'm ninety-nine percent sure that I've found the location of the man who ordered the attack.

I hit call on the nameless number in Edgar's phone.

"Is it done?" a man answers.

Jesus, this is too easy.

"Yep, I killed every single one of your pathetic men."

Silence.

I think he might have hung up, but apparently, this idiot really thought he had a chance to bring me down.

"Now that I have your attention..." I brush the dirt off my nails, barely even thinking about this conversation. My voice holds enough of a threat to let this man know that I'm serious. "...you will not attack me again.

"I now have men monitoring your every movement. If you do anything out of the ordinary, if I suspect in any way that you are going to attack and come after me again, then I will have you killed. Along with everyone who works for you, everyone you love, everyone you've ever met. Do you understand, Mr. Tirkel?" I say as I pull up the name associated with his number on my computer.

He's speechless, but his breathing is heavy and nasally, so I know he's still on the line.

"Mr. Tirkel? I need confirmation that you heard me."

"I—uh—I heard you."

"This is your only warning. And you should know that I don't give warnings often. The only reason you are getting one is because I don't want to bother with sending someone to kill you. That's how little you mean to me. But make one wrong step and I will."

"Yes, I understand."

"Good. And oh, Mr. Tirkel? Next time you try to take down a stronger man than yourself, don't send your men in to fight for you. Grow some balls, man up and fight yourself. If you're not capable of doing that, then you shouldn't order the attack in the first place."

I hang up the phone, putting no more thought to Mr. Tirkel.

He's an idiot with no skills and no money. He won't be attacking again. His attempt smelt of desperation. He needed money for his organization so badly that he was willing to try me.

I lean my head back again. The sun has begun to set.

I have a choice to make. Stay here with Phoenix and hope that Liesel obeys me by coming back tomorrow, or go out and search for Liesel myself before she slips through my fingers.

I'm pretty sure Liesel isn't coming back. She may want answers, but she's too stubborn to listen to anything I say. I should have told her to never come back, and then she might show up on my front door tomorrow.

But I'm not one hundred percent sure. She's tired of the lies too. She wants answers as much as I do. Although, we each have our own reasons for wanting answers.

I give her a ten percent chance of coming back on her own.

I won't go hunt her.

I'll wait and let her make her move. I'll let her decide her fate. If she comes back, I'll be more lenient on her. But if she runs...my brain fills with all the things it wants to do to her.

I won't be doing any of them. I'll do the smart thing. The thing that hits her where it hurts and gives me what I want.

I should get up and go talk to Phoenix. Just five more minutes of relaxing and then I'll go to her.

A lightbulb goes off in my head.

I know what Liesel's going to do.

I pull out my phone and stare at the names of all the contacts Liesel knows in our dangerous world.

Enzo.

Kai.

Zeke.

Siren.

Who would she call for help?

The answer is obvious. She knows me better than anyone, but I know her better than anyone too.

I dial Siren's number.

"I'm not going to help you keep Liesel hostage. If you want to talk, you can talk to Zeke. I'm not talking to you until you let her go," Siren huffs into the phone.

"Wait!" I say before she can hand the phone off to Zeke.

"You have three seconds."

"Liesel is going to call you for help."

There's a silent beat before she answers. "What do you want me to do?"

"Help her."

3
LIESEL

"THAT FUCKING BASTARD! I'll have a plane there in two hours," Siren says when I finish telling her everything.

I let out an audible breath.

I'm getting rescued.

"Thank you."

"Of course. And don't worry, Langston is going to get a mouthful from me next time I see him. He's an asshole for thinking he can just kidnap you like that, even if he'd never actually kill you. He's just trying to bully and intimidate you into doing what he wants."

I can't wipe the smile off my face.

"You have no idea how much I appreciate your help. I'll pay you back—"

"Don't you dare. You have nothing to pay me back for."

"Not even by going with you on a girls trip?"

I can feel her smile through the phone. "Kai would kill me if I didn't use this opportunity to persuade you to go on a girls trip with us, but I don't think persuasion will be necessary. You'll want to vent after all of this is over."

"You're probably right." I won't be venting to Waylon about my time here, that's for sure.

"Hang tight. I'll have you off his island in two hours." Siren hangs up the phone.

Two hours until I'm free.

I stare down the road that leads toward Langston's house as the sun begins to rise. Even if Langston comes for me before I'm rescued, I trust Siren. She'll find me and make Langston release me.

This is truly the end of this nightmare.

Wait...

I didn't give Siren my location. *How does she know where I am? And where am I exactly?*

I shake off the weird vibes. She probably just knows because she knows where Langston has been living lately and the location of his beach house. I'm sure he's told those he's close to before. I'm just not one of those people anymore.

I sit back down in my hut and wait.

The sun has fully risen when I hear the roar of an engine. I step out of the hut, hoping I'm not dreaming up the sound of the airplane and it's not just Langston's car or another attack.

I refuse to think about who those men are or why they were attacking Langston. It's been a while since I've heard any explosions or gunfire—not a good sign. That means Langston is no longer occupied by fighting. He could be searching for me.

I shield my eyes and look up.

A plane.

I hold my breath while the plane lands, begging it to be Siren's team.

Finally, the plane rolls to a stop, and the side door lowers. Siren sticks her head out the doorway.

I exhale. She's here. I wish she had sent a team to pick me up instead of doing it herself, but I'm happy that she's here. It means I'm getting off this island and away from Langston for good.

"Any sign of Lanston?" Siren asks as I jog toward the plane.

I shake my head.

"Good, let's get going before he figures out I'm here. I'll deal with his dumb ass later."

I smile.

Siren pulls me into a hug even though I'm covered in dried dirt, leaves, and sweat.

I wince when she hugs me too tightly, agitating the wound on the back of my shoulder.

"I'm sorry, are you okay?" Siren asks as she holds me at arm's length and looks me up and down.

"It's okay; I've been sleeping on the jungle floor. I'm just sore." I don't want her to know I'm wounded. I want her to know as little as possible.

She nods. "There is a bathroom in the back with a small shower. The water won't stay hot for long, but you can at least clean up. I'll put a change of clothes outside the bathroom door for you."

"Thanks, looking forward to getting off this island."

"I'll go talk to the pilot and get us out of here as soon as possible. Be careful showering during takeoff."

"Of course." Although, I'm not worried about getting knocked around during takeoff. I've been through hell; a possible bruise as I bump into the shower door is nothing.

I walk to the back of the plane and find a small bathroom. I don't know whose private jet this is—probably Enzo and Kai's. Siren and Zeke have money, but I don't think they own their own private jet to my knowledge. Or she chartered this.

The bathroom is just big enough for one person to fit in. It has a small sink, toilet, and corner shower. I take my clothes off, letting them fall to the floor. I don't dare look at myself in the mirror. If I did, I'm not sure whether I'd see a strong, determined woman or a frail, broken one.

Instead, I flip the water on and step under the spray. The water is cool; I don't bother letting it heat up. I don't need it to be warm. Siren also said it won't stay warm for long anyway.

I let the water wash away the mud, the dried leaves, the blood from the bug bites and scratches. It also cleanses me of my pain and anger.

I can't believe Langston kidnapped me. I can't believe he threatened my life—all for a secret treasure he doesn't even need. He has his own private island and mansion. He doesn't need money. He just wants to hurt me.

We've been through a lot as kids, but I still feel like there is something I'm missing, something Langston is hiding. His rage goes far beyond the truth as I know it.

I feel the plane rising off the ground.

My body lightens, as if a weight has been lifted from my body as we takeoff.

I don't have to worry about Langston anymore. I don't have to spend another second thinking about him.

Fuck Langston and his stupid games. Siren won't let him come near me again.

I hear a light tapping on the door. I'm sure it's just Siren telling me she put clothes outside the door for me.

I don't stop showering, though, until I've used every

ounce of water. Even then, I let the water droplets drip down my hair, face, and body.

I stare at these little miracles—tiny water droplets that brought me back to life.

After several minutes, I can't hide in the bathroom anymore. I dry off and wrap a towel around me before cracking the door open to grab the clothes Siren left for me.

I look at them closely—jeans and a black T-shirt, fighting clothes. I quickly change, even though my hips don't fill out the jeans like Siren's would. My breasts fill the shirt, stretching the material to its limit.

I run my hand through my wet hair—good enough.

When I step out in the main cabin, I find Siren sitting in a chair holding Cayden.

How did I miss her baby when I entered?

I was too worried about just getting on the plane and in the shower to wash off everything that happened.

"Feel better?" Siren asks with a tense smile.

"Yes, thank you." I make my way over to the captain's chair directly across from her and sit down. Cayden is asleep in her arms, and Siren seems content to just let him sleep there.

"Is Zeke here?"

She shakes her head. "It's just me, Cayden, and the pilot."

"What if Langston had gotten to me first?"

"You don't think I'm capable of getting Langston to do whatever I say?" Her eyes twinkle, and her face lightens with the knowledge that she's able to control a man she's not even married to.

My ribs clench, and my stomach drops in jealousy. If only I could control Langston as easily. It makes me wish even more that Siren wasn't here.

I stare out the window as we fly over the ocean. I'm not

even sure where we are. I'm about to ask, but Siren beats me to speaking.

"This plane can take you anywhere. So, where are we going?" Siren asks.

I furrow my brows as I glance back to her. *We* aren't going anywhere. I'll only be able to stand Siren until this plane ride is over, and then I'll need her to head back to Zeke.

"Home."

Siren blinks rapidly, trying to digest my single word in disbelief. She sits up and slowly lifts Cayden off her lap, placing him on the couch across from us. Once he's solidly asleep again, she folds her arms and stares down at me like she's about to give me an order.

"New York? You can't go back there."

"Why not? It's my home. It's where I want to be." I stand up, wanting to be on the same eye level as her. I won't let her, or anyone else, bully me into feeling weak.

"That will be the first place Langston looks!"

I glance at Cayden as Siren raises her voice, but he sleeps right through it. I guess when you grow up in our world, you can sleep through anything.

"I'm not going to run anymore. I'm not going to play his games."

"Just hide out, take a vacation somewhere until I can talk some sense into that boy."

"No. I have Waylon to worry about. I have a job. A life. I'm not going to let Langston take anything more from me."

Siren's eyes flick side to side as she looks into my eyes, hoping to find something in my eyes to persuade me. She won't find anything. My decision is already made.

She lets out a long breath, blowing some of her hair out of her eyes.

"I'll tell the pilot we are headed for New York, and then you and I are going to talk."

She heads toward the front of the plane, while I take a seat again, feeling victorious, even though I know she's not going to let this go that easily. I close my eyes. Maybe if I pretend to sleep, Siren will ignore me.

"Nuh-uh. That's not going to work. You're not asleep. Start talking," Siren says as she plops back into her chair.

My eyes flick open. "I can't."

"Why not?"

"It's a long story."

"We've got time."

I close my eyes again. "Sorry, Siren. I don't want to lie to you, and that's all I'll do if I start talking. You're better off not knowing."

I texted Waylon to meet me at my apartment, but I never got a response. I don't know if he'll be here or not. I don't know if he called the police and filed a missing person report. I don't know if he's given up on me coming back.

I get to my apartment door and realize I don't have my key. I knock, hoping Waylon is inside, so I don't have to break into my own apartment.

I hear footsteps inside, and I fidget with the hem of my black T-shirt. *Will Waylon notice that I'm not wearing my usual power dress? Will he know that something's instantly wrong? Will he ask me a dozen questions about where I've been or what I've been up to?*

What do I tell him? How do I keep him safe?

The door swings open—the moment of reckoning.

"Baby, I didn't think you were getting back from your trip for a while. I'm so happy you decided to change your plans and head home early." He grabs me by the back of my neck and kisses me in a friendly kiss. His tongue parts my lips, his hand massages my neck, and he moans softly against my lips. It's a good kiss—a grateful kiss, but not an 'I was worried you were kidnapped, murdered, or dropped off the face of the earth' kiss.

"Yep, I missed you. Thought I'd come back early."

Waylon pulls me tightly to him, until I'm pressed up against him. That's when I get a whiff of him—a musky, sweaty scent. I scan him up and down and realize he's in a T-shirt and gym shorts. He must have just worked out.

"We are going to have to celebrate later, though. How about Noda for dinner in three hours? I need to shower, and then I have a quick meeting. After that, I'm all yours." He wiggles his eyebrows suggestively.

My body melts at his proposal. I need to let off some steam, and fucking Waylon all night is just the way to do it.

Waylon notices my body's reaction. He leans in and kisses me softly on the lips. The kiss is full of promise for tonight.

I want to protest and tell him I want him now, but a knock at the door interrupts my plea.

We both groan in annoyance at whoever is at the door, who interrupted our kiss.

"I really need to shower and get to my meeting. Soon, love," Waylon says, and then he's jogging down the hallway to the bathroom.

I turn to the door, hoping it's just a delivery. If it's Siren, I'm going to kill her.

I open the door.

Langston is standing in the hallway with a heavy scowl, dark eyes, and an evil grin twisted on his face.

"I told you to come find me," he growls.

My stomach drops as he pushes his way into my apartment and back into my world in record time. There is no getting rid of him, not unless I kill him.

"Waylon is in the shower. You can't stay."

"Good. It's time I find out the truth. If he's here, you won't be able to lie about the status of your marriage."

4
LANGSTON

As I STEP CLOSER to Liesel, she retreats—backing away, but not backing down. Her scowl and ridges between her eyes shoot through my body. She doesn't want me here.

Well, too bad. I don't want to be here either.

If she hadn't forced my hand, if she'd at the very least stayed on the island, then I wouldn't be invading her apartment with her supposed husband in the next room.

I kick the door closed behind me, purposefully slamming it.

"Shh," Liesel hisses.

I tilt my head. "Why? Worried dear old hubby will notice?"

"Don't make fun of Waylon."

"I'm not making fun of him. I just can't imagine you're married to that fossil."

"I am," she says without hesitation, with as much conviction as she can muster.

"Well, that's the problem—I don't believe a word you say."

She shrugs. "That's not my problem. Now get out of my house."

"We had a deal."

"No, you kidnapped me and forced me to agree to your terms. So unless you're planning on kidnapping me again, we're done here."

Oh, I plan on kidnapping her again if I need to. But I'll take my time. First, I want answers. Then I can worry about what I'm going to do with her.

"It doesn't matter if you're on the island or not. Our deal remains. You will tell me truths, and I'll give you more time to live. You tell me lies, and I'll give you less time. You're down to eleven months. I took off a month after you ran and made me come after you. Now's your chance to earn some time back."

Liesel glances down the hallway as she bites her bottom lip. The shower is still running, so we have some time before Waylon joins us.

"Did Siren rat me out?" Liesel asks.

No, she didn't. But I won't let Liesel think she has any friends on her side. Liesel needs to know that she's all alone battling me.

I'll have to deal with Siren later, though. I can't have her intervening in my plan. It's probably time I told Siren the truth. Then I wouldn't have to worry about whose side she's on. She would be firmly on mine.

"Of course. You really think you could turn one of my best friends so easily?"

Her eyes narrow, searching for the truth in my eyes. In my words. In my body language.

I don't let my anger rise beyond my gut. I don't let my voice carry my pain. I don't let my eyes widen in worry.

Liesel sighs. "Maybe not, but she freed me. She's clearly not as close to you as you think."

I chuckle and step closer to her, forcing her to step back. "You think you're free?"

"I'm in my own damn house, and as soon as Waylon gets out of the shower, he'll kick your ass if you don't leave."

"Will he?" I take another step, and her back hits the wall.

She glares as she pushes past me and heads into the kitchen. She winces when her injured shoulder brushes against mine.

I stare at her back, wanting to ask about her wound. To take a look at it and make sure it's healing properly. To remove the staples.

But that would show that I care. It would be a weak move. And I'm tired of being powerless for this woman.

I storm after her, not letting her even catch her breath or grab a knife, which I assume is the only reason she's heading into the kitchen.

I cock my head and smirk at her as she pulls a knife out of a cutting block. "Really? You think a knife is going to protect you? You're so predictable."

"No, a knife won't protect me against a monster like you. You don't play fair. And you're more skilled at killing people than anyone I've ever met. If you want me dead, you'll kill me."

"Then why even bother grabbing it? Why fight me? Why not just tell me the truth? You'll live a longer, much happier life if you just give in," I say, standing on one side of the kitchen island. She stands on the other side, using the island as a barrier between us.

"You don't deserve the truth, killer. You don't get any more parts of me."

"But I haven't even gotten to taste the best part yet." My voice is low and throaty as I speak.

I swear I hear Liesel gasp.

We may both be married, but that doesn't extinguish the fire between us. That doesn't stop the pull of attraction. No matter how much Liesel hurts me, no matter how much she betrays me, on some level, my body will always want her. I just have to remember she's poison to me. One taste and she'll eviscerate me.

"You stole a kiss against my will—you don't get more. I'll cut off your balls if you so much as touch me without permission."

There's my feisty huntress.

I laugh. "I don't have to take anything—before I'm done with you, you'll be willingly giving in to me. You'll be begging me to kiss you, to fuck you."

"I have a wonderful husband just down the hall who is more than capable of satisfying my every need. He kisses like a king and makes me come like a servant. Why would I need a schmuck like you? You wouldn't even be able to find my clit."

Her words are firm and defiant, but I notice her chest heaving up and down. She's all hot and bothered inside. I remember the explosive orgasms she had with Waylon. I remember the sounds she made, the faces. *How much of that was real and how much of that was fake?*

"Now you make me wonder if Waylon is the one who doesn't know where your clit is."

"Just like Phoenix doesn't know how to suck you off, huh?"

Her eyes glitter with jealousy. She doesn't like that I'm married to Phoenix any more than I like her marriage to Waylon. Not because I want to be married to her, but because she's mine. She doesn't get to belong to anyone else.

"I'd be happy to let you try if you think you can do better. But let me tell you, no one sucks me off like Phoenix."

Her grip on the thin knife tightens, along with the lines around her eyes and harsh frown of her lips.

"Just leave; neither of us is going to tell the truth. We aren't going to say that we lied and that we aren't married.

That you don't have any freaking kids. Just go. We don't have to keep hurting each other."

I take a step toward her, expecting her step away from me, keeping the island between us.

She doesn't.

"You really think you're going to stab me if I get near?"

"You'll have to come closer to find out." She smirks and twists the knife around casually in her hand like it belongs there.

She forgets that I know the real her. She doesn't like wielding a weapon. The only time she holds a knife is when she's cutting into her food. She wouldn't even be able to flick her wrist in my direction before my reflexes would stop her without even thinking.

I take another step.

She still doesn't move.

My heart beats wildly in my chest, wanting to be near her, even though the only part of me that Liesel could actually damage is my heart. She has no idea the amount of torture she's caused me. She thinks I'm the devil. I am, but I have nothing on her.

One more step and I'm standing face to face in front of her.

Her breathing is erratic. I can't tell if she's scared or turned on.

"Are. You. Married?" I ask. If she is, then she could go after the treasure without me. I want to know for my own personal reasons. I want to know so I know how to destroy her.

"I already told you I am."

"You sure about that?" I study her for any signs that she's telling the truth or lying, but all I can focus on his her breathing in and out. Her chest is rising and falling beneath Siren's black T-shirt.

"Yes," she says sharply, expecting me to call her out.

I inch closer, just leaning into her personal space. I won't touch her without her permission or invitation, but I can do a lot without touching her. And I'm not planning on leaving until I get this single truth.

I take a deep breath, breathing in her scent—lavender and something floral. When I exhale down her neck, I watch her shiver.

I put my hands in the pockets of my jeans to keep from touching her.

Not yet.

Soon, though, I'll be able to touch her.

It won't take long to break her—to get her begging to be touched.

My eyes run down her body from head to toe. I linger over her hair—long and wavy and slightly frizzier than usual, untamed. My eyes heat over the curves of her breasts and hips and then down her slim legs to her oversized boots. She doesn't look like the Liesel I've known all my life. She's not wearing the right clothes, and her makeup isn't caked on. But somehow, standing there with that damn knife in her hand, she's never looked more incredible.

My eyes snap back up, meeting hers.

She shivers once again.

"Cold?"

"Hmm."

I shrug my jacket off and drape it over her shoulders. I let my fingers graze her arms as I pull the jacket tighter in front of her. My hands grip her hips before I even realize I'm touching her.

"Better?" I ask.

"Hmm."

I've made her speechless. Although, I'm not much better. I only got one word out.

I have to take back control. I can't let her affect me. I have to beat her at her own game.

I lick my lips.

Her mouth parts.

The air changes—she's in a daze.

"Kiss me," she says suddenly.

She's lost her mind, but she doesn't have to tell me twice.

I press my lips against hers, reveling in how incredible her soft lips feel against mine. But I'm greedy, and I want more than just the softness. I want the taste of her sweetness, the battle of her tongue with mine, the moans she makes when I make her feel alive.

This kiss is just as mind-blowing as our last kiss and so much more. This kiss isn't about chasing demons away. This kiss is about need, desire, want. It's about taking back what's mine.

I don't give a damn if Liesel is married or not. I can steal her back either way.

"Tell me to stop," I say against her lips.

"Sss..." She doesn't make it past the first letter before she's kissing me again.

I smirk against her lips, slowing her kisses. As much as I would love to lose myself in this kiss, I can't. I'm here on a mission, and I won't let earth-shattering kisses stand in my way.

"So, you're a cheater, then?" I ask as I pull her hips tightly against mine, pressing my hardness against her jeans.

"Huh?" she moans.

"You have an open marriage? Waylon doesn't mind you kissing strange men?"

"What? No."

She puts her empty hand against my chest.

"Tell me to stop," I repeat.

She breathes hard and fast, her lips devouring over mine.

She rocks back and forward, letting our hips rub before falling back.

She wants this.

She wants *me*.

But something is holding her back. Is she really married? Is she just dating that asshole? Does she not care about him at all?

"Sto…" She takes a deep breath. "Stop."

"That took far too long for a married woman. Unless you don't mind being a cheater?"

"I'm not a cheater," she growls, getting her voice back.

"You're the one who asked me to kiss you." I don't back away. My hands are still on her hips, and hers are now both on my chest, still holding the knife. But she doesn't push me away. She lets me stay close.

"I. Am. Not. A. Cheater."

"Then you're not married?"

Liesel looks at me with a fierceness in her eyes. She's about to try and use the knife on me because she's pissed I won. That I got in her head and got me to kiss her.

Just like I knew she would, she throws her arms up, trying to strike me with the knife in the neck. But I catch her wrist and hold the knife suspended in the air between us.

Her face is locked on mine. She's trying to be a shell. She's trying to keep her emotions off her face, but I notice the lift of her lips in a hint of a smile before her lip quivers, and her eyes widen.

"Please," she trembles.

My eyes search hers for answers. *Why did she just flip a switch? How did she go from lust to anger to fear in three seconds?*

"Get your hands off my wife," Waylon says from behind me.

And then Liesel can't keep the smirk off her face. It flashes for only a second. Only long enough for me to notice, but not long enough for Waylon to see it.

She got the knife to frame me.

She asked me to kiss her to force me close, so that in Waylon's eyes, it looks like I'm attacking her.

I have a decision to make. *Do I let her win—go and walk out the door? Or do I fight back?*

Liesel knows that if I wanted to take down Waylon right now, I could. *Did she just sign Waylon's death sentence, all for a chance to beat me?*

"We aren't finished. I'll let you win this round, but I still want answers. And your time is running out. You have twenty-four hours to decide if you want to finish the game here or back on my island. But remember whom you are risking if you choose to finish our game here," I whisper so only she can hear.

I let go of her arm.

I half expect when I turn around for Waylon to have a gun pointed at my head. For him to be holding a bat, something.

Instead, he's standing there in a suit. His graying hair is slicked back, and there is a drop of blood on his jawline from where he cut himself shaving.

"I called the police. Get out if you don't want to spend the rest of your life in jail," Waylon says.

I shake my head. *Lawyers—they are all the same.* Cocky smart-alecks who think the police will step in and save them. They don't know that if the police showed up, they'd just look the other way as soon as I paid them off or whispered my name.

The only thing protecting Waylon right now is that I want to know who Waylon truly is to Liesel before I kill him. Whether he's truly her husband, the love of her life, or just a man she fucks because she's lonely. I'll figure it out.

I don't speak as I walk out the door like a stranger back into the night. The man isn't worth my words.

The door slams behind me. A heaviness weighs me down as I ride the elevator down.

Wife.

Waylon called Liesel his wife.

She had to have warned him before I got here to call her that, to pretend they are married. *Right?*

Liesel Dunn can't be married.

Can't. Be.

My steel heart hardens. It won't break. It won't even crack. Not for her.

Liesel may think Waylon calling her his wife is confirmation that she's married, but it's not. I want her to tell me the truth. Sure, I could look up her marriage license with the city, *but what fun is that?*

No, after her little stunt, I'm going to pull every truth I can from her, until the truth kills her.

5
LIESEL

LANGSTON WALKS OUT THE DOOR, and then it slams shut.

I stand frozen—pretending I'm in shock. I am, but not because Langston threatened my life. In fact, he offered to give me more time if I told him the truth. He gave me a chance to save my life if only I answered one question.

The only problem is that I don't know the answer because I don't know the question. I don't know what specific truth matters above all others. The one that matters beyond the secrets only I know from the ripped paper.

None of that is the reason I'm in shock.

That fucking kiss.

Waylon runs over to me and consumes me in his muscular arms, yanking me against his hard chest.

"Shh, I've got you. I've got you. I won't let that man or anyone hurt you," Waylon says.

I should feel safe with his arms around me. His thick chest is as protective as any armor. His soothing voice normally eases my tensions.

Instead, I feel rattled. My body trembles, and I feel empty.

My brain is trying to process Waylon's words. I'm trying to come up with a plan to explain Langston to Waylon. To figure out how to defeat Langston while keeping myself and Waylon safe.

But.

That.

Kiss.

I planned it, knowing that it would knock Langston off balance. It would bring him in close and help me set a trap where Waylon would find us close.

But I was the one knocked askew as soon as our lips touched. The spark at our touch took hold of every nerve ending and brain cell in my body. The entire time he was kissing me, I forgot about my plan. I forgot that Langston is the enemy.

"You're trembling. It's okay, baby. Try to take a deep breath. You're safe," Waylon says.

He doesn't realize that I'm not safe. I'm never safe.

I take a deep breath—trying to shake the sparks still shooting off my body. My adrenaline is up, which is probably why I'm shaking. I crave more kisses, more of his touch, just more.

I won. I won't let the memories of Langston take the victory from me. He doesn't get to win by taking my thoughts, my cravings, my body.

I grip onto Waylon's forearms while I lean back, looking into his eyes.

He smiles down at me sweetly. He really is a sweet, kind-hearted man. He's what I need, not Langston.

"Kiss me," I whisper. I meant to speak stronger, more assertively, but I'm too shaken up. As much as I want to get rid of Langston's touch, I also want to wallow in it, no matter how much pain it will eventually bring me. I don't want to forget Langston's kiss, but I need to.

Waylon, who can never deny me, leans down and plants the softest kiss, barely brushing his lips against mine. That won't be enough to wipe Langston from my memory.

I reach up, grabbing onto his sculpted neck and parting his lips with my tongue, pushing deep inside his mouth, begging for him to kiss me with all of his passion.

Waylon takes the hint. He's so perceptive, always listening to the little clues I give him.

He pushes me back until my ass is against the counter. His hands grip my hips firmly but not in a controlling way. His thick, hard muscles push against me until I feel his cock pressing against my stomach. His tongue sweeps in my mouth, commanding my attention as it dances over mine.

I should feel that all-consuming, heart-stopping, breathless emotion. That emotion one step below love or, at the very least, deep lust.

This kiss is barely getting my heart thumping, though. My body didn't come alive. The spark didn't fan into flames. And worst of all, it didn't wipe any memory of Langston's kiss from my brain, my body, my heart.

Langston is just a good kisser. That's all it is.

There is no way a man like that kissed me while married. If he is married, he sure as hell isn't in love. You can't kiss another woman if you love your wife.

"Liesel?" Waylon asks, searching my eyes for my thoughts as he pulls away.

I shake off the memories, but that will only last for a moment at best before Langston will weasel his way back into my head. It's clear Waylon must have asked me a question, but I didn't hear it.

"Sorry, I'm still a little frazzled. What did you say?"

Waylon's hands are still on me, afraid I'll fall to pieces. He's probably right, but it's because of that damn kiss, not because I had a knife pressed against my neck.

"Can you tell me what happened before I actually call the police?" Waylon asks.

I take a deep breath as I prepare the lie. "There was a knock at the door after you went to the shower. I assumed it was a package being delivered. When I opened the door, he grabbed me and held a knife to my throat. He told me he wanted money and information about your campaign plans. And then you walked in."

"Oh, baby. I'm so sorry." Waylon pulls me to him again.

"It's okay. I'm okay now, but I think we should hire some security." Security won't stop Langston, but it might slow him down.

Waylon nods. "I agree. I'll double the amount of security we were planning. And I think we should start my campaign for governor as soon as possible. Actually being on the campaign trail will make a statement to those trying to attack us that we aren't afraid. That we have security who will protect us and throw any criminal who comes at us in jail."

"I don't think we should call the police."

"Why not?" Waylon wrinkles his forehead.

"We don't want anyone to know we were attacked. Our security team can find the man who did this without a public investigation."

His eyes roll up for a minute, and then he lets out an exacerbated breath. "You're right. It just means you can't go anywhere without security or me by your side. No more answering doors by yourself. Are you okay with that?"

I suck in a breath. *No, I'm not okay with that.* It means giving up control to someone else, relying on someone else for protection. It's what I did when I was part of Enzo's gang of minions. I vowed to never do it again.

But this isn't about keeping me safe, not really. It's about doing everything I can to protect Waylon.

"I understand."

Waylon's raised shoulders relax as he exhales.

"You have no idea how terrified I was watching that man hold a knife to your throat. I never want to be that scared again. I'd give up everything—my work, my campaign, my money, my life to never have you threatened again. I can't lose you, my love."

I put my arms around Waylon. "I can't lose you either."

He kisses the top of my head in a move that's meant to make me feel safe and loved—two things I've never been.

"I need to make some calls. You going to be okay?"

I nod. "I'm going to shower. Then you can talk to me about your plans for our security and your first campaign events."

"I'm so lucky I have you."

"Me too."

Then I walk down the hallway to the bathroom.

I close the bathroom door and take a deep breath as I slink to the floor. I close my eyes, trying to push Langston out, but he floods my head.

His hands on mine.

His body pressed against mine.

His lips…

STOP! I can't think about any of that.

Langston's body is replaced by his words in my mind. He said I have twenty-four hours to decide if I want to finish the game here or back on his island. But if I choose to finish our game here, he threatened Waylon.

I don't want to risk Waylon's life, but it's not about choosing between keeping him safe or not. Langston will hang Waylon's life over me no matter where I fight Langston.

This is about choosing between the two men. *Who do I trust? Whose side do I want to be on?*

The choice is easy—Waylon.

It has to be Waylon. I can't choose Langston.

All that's left to do is to convince my body it wants Waylon, not Langston.

I shower and get dressed.

I listen while Waylon talks to me about hiring security and starting his campaign.

Then I kiss him goodnight. I should fuck him, remind my body whom it craves.

I can't.

I'm exhausted, and my body is buzzing for another man. I need space and time. Only then will I be able to reconnect with Waylon.

"I'm here if you need me, but I need to finish some calls before I come to bed," Waylon says.

"I'm going to take a long, relaxing bath, and then I'll meet you in bed."

"You deserve to relax."

I walk to the bathroom and start filling the tub when my cell phone rings.

If it's Siren or Kai, I'm not answering. I'm pissed at Siren for ratting me out, and I don't want Kai's sympathy. If it's anyone calling about any of Waylon's plans, I'm too tired to listen.

I stare at the name. I intended to turn the phone off, to not answer.

But with one flash of his name, my heart skips, and my insides warm.

My thumb hovers over the button.

Just turn it off. Turn off the phone and enjoy your bath.

Somehow, my thumb brushes against the answer button. I bring the phone up to my ear, and I speak.

6
LANGSTON

LIESEL ANSWERS THE PHONE.

I wasn't sure if she would or if I would have to sneak over in the middle of the night to drag her out of bed and force her to talk to me.

"Hello," her voice is breathy as she answers.

"Have you decided? Are we finishing this here or on the island?"

She shakes her head on my monitor screen. I'm watching her from my hotel room across the street from her building. "Really? We aren't even going to talk about the fact that I tricked you and won? How does your *wife* feel about you kissing me?"

"My wife is none of your concern," I snap back.

She turns off the tub faucet but keeps the phone near her ear.

"I have eighteen hours left to decide according to you. I won't give you an answer until then."

"But you've already decided."

She frowns but doesn't speak, which only confirms my guess.

"Are we done? I'm sure you'll find me when my twenty-four-hours are up so you can get my answer then."

"We aren't done."

"I would like to enjoy some peace and quiet, so can we hurry this along?"

"Why? Anxious to get into that bath so you can touch yourself to the memory of our kiss?" My voice is a low, deep timbre that practically vibrates through the phone and down her body.

She shivers at my words.

"You're watching me?"

"Yes," I hum.

More shivers. Her cheeks pink. Her eyes search the bathroom.

"Where did you put the camera?"

"Does it matter? Are you planning on putting on a show for me?"

"I'm planning on showing you what you will never have."

She grabs the hem of her black T-shirt, stretches it over her body, and then her breasts are staring back at me.

Fuck, I shouldn't have called her when she was headed into the bathroom. I'm not going to be able to concentrate on pulling the truth from her when her body looks like that—smooth, curvy, and welcoming.

I close my eyes when I see her start on her jeans, but they only stayed closed less than a second. Then they are glued to the screen, watching her jeans slide to the floor, followed by her panties.

She's standing naked in the bathroom with the phone still to her ear. "I hope your wife walks in and sees how hard I make you. I hope she slaps you and takes all of your money before she leaves your cheating ass."

"I don't cheat."

"So you aren't really married, then?"

A beat passes.

She smiles like she won again before she steps into the tub. Her body disappears under the water's surface while resting her head against the tub's edge.

I exhale—her spell on me breaks as she slips under the water, her body no longer as visible to me.

"We are going to continue our little game. You tell me the truth, and I give you more time to live. You tell me a lie, and I give you less time. I don't care if we are here or back on the island. The battle continues until I pull every last truth from you, or you run out of time."

She smirks, her seductive eyes glancing up, looking right at me. "What makes you think I'll answer you? I'm not your captive anymore."

"Because I'll start hurting and killing people you care about. And I'll automatically take a month off your time every time you don't answer me. Your time will run out very quickly if you don't start talking."

She closes her eyes and leans her head back on the back of the edge of the tub. "What do you want to know?"

I was expecting more of a fight. Apparently, I've knocked all the fight out of her, at least for tonight.

"Tell me the truth of how you and Waylon met."

She keeps her eyes closed, which makes it hard for me to read her expression or emotion. When she does finally speak, the tone of her voice is my only clue as to whether or not she's telling the truth. Doing this from a distance is going to be difficult.

"A blind date," she finally says.

I narrow my eyes, trying to read her.

Her eyes softly open. "We are both lawyers. We run in the same circles. We have mutual friends. Waylon was looking to settle down, for someone serious to help him build a long-lasting political career where he could make a difference. I was looking for a partner with power to keep me safe from men like you."

I laugh at her comment about Waylon being able to protect her. I don't even think Liesel believes that. Even if Waylon could keep her safe, she wouldn't want that. She wants to control her own safety.

"You really think Waylon can protect you?"

"He has power—that's as much protection as I can expect from a man."

At least that's the truth.

"What did you do on your first date?"

Liesel adjusts herself in the tub, and I get a glimmer of cleavage as she lifts slightly out of the water. My cock throbs at the sight.

"The usual drinks at a bar and then dinner at a nice Italian restaurant."

"Was it love at first sight?"

She laughs as she sinks back into the water. "He ordered my drink and meal for me. What do you think?"

"I think you castrated him right then and there." I smile just imagining what Liesel would do if a man tried to control her like that. *But then how did she end up married to the ass?*

"I ordered the most expensive champagne on the menu, and then I threw it at him."

"Not scotch?"

She scoffs. "Would I ever waste scotch?"

My smile grows to my eyes. I haven't smiled this big in a long time. It almost feels like we are kids teasing each other again—almost.

"No, I don't imagine you ever would."

Liesel smiles so openly I can see every one of her white teeth. It makes me almost not want to ask her my next question, but I need to know.

"What happened next? How did you end up on a second date if the first date ended in such a disaster?"

Her smile immediately drops from her face, almost as if it was never there in the first place. She takes her time before she speaks, the movie of those events flashing before her eyes.

She's trying to decide if she tells me the truth or if she tells me a lie.

"You lose two weeks from your life if you lie," I warn.

"I was at a bar. A man sat down next to me and started up a conversation with me," her voice is soft, and her bottom lip trembles as she speaks.

I hate this man, whoever he is instantly.

"The man seemed nice enough. He was a typical suit—nicely groomed, a banker with warm eyes. He was charming, and I was lonely and frustrated with my lack of a sex life, so we got a hotel room."

Jesus, so many awful things happen to this woman. It's like she's a magnet for evil men.

"In the elevator on the way up, I started to get some bad vibes from him. I made a phone call and said I had to go..."

Her voice trails off as she looks down at her hands like she's embarrassed.

"He was in the wrong, not you," I say, trying to make her feel better before I realize that's not my job.

The corner of her mouth lifts in gratitude for my words. "He forced me into the hotel room. Ripped my clothes. Tried to rape me."

"Tried?" My heart stops.

"The call was to Waylon. He was the only person I could think of who might be close. He was an asshole, but I didn't get the same vibes from Waylon as I did from Frank."

"He rescued you?"

"Sort of. I was able to knee him in the balls and break free."

I smile, knowing I was the one who taught her that move.

"Waylon was in the lobby by the time I made it down. He called the police. We went and got some greasy burger and fries from a dive next door. He made me laugh. He tried to protect me."

She gave Waylon a second chance. *Why could she never give me one?*

I sigh.

"How did you and Phoenix meet?" Liesel asks.

"I picked her up at a club. She was the only woman, not on the dance floor, trying to get my attention."

She smiles again, happy that I'm talking.

"I fucked her in the dirty bathroom. It was the hottest sex of my life. Nine months later, she had our first child."

Liesel's smile snaps off her face, replaced by a scowl. "Liar."

I hear the hope in her voice. She doesn't truly believe I'm lying, she just hopes I am. Whether she will ever admit it or not, she wants me. It hurts her to hear that I'm with another woman, especially one related to her.

I don't care if she believes me or not. What I care about is figuring out if she's lying. I don't think she is, but I also don't think she's telling the full truth.

"Do you trust Waylon?"

"Not going to ask if I love him?"

"I don't care if you love him or not," I lie. "I care if you trust him."

"He's my husband."

"That's not an answer."

"I've already answered my question for tonight," she says, dodging the question.

Interesting.

"Last chance to tell me why, Liesel. I'm done asking. This is your last chance to save your life. Just give me one good reason for what you did and this can all be over. I'll leave you alone, if that's what you want. You'll never hear from me or see me again. Just tell me why," I say.

I'm so completely desperate. I need this answer more than I need anything else. I would trade all of her truths for this one single bit of information. I'll give her up; I just need to know why. I need to know why she did the cruelest thing that anyone in our group has ever done. We all work for a criminal organization; we've done some fucked up shit, but nothing like what Liesel did.

"Why?" I repeat.

She blinks; it's the only clue I have that she even heard me. She looks right at me, finding the camera. "I have no clue what you are talking about. Maybe if you'd ask me an actual question, I would answer you."

I run my hand through my hair in frustration. I need to know, but her refusing means I get to keep her. I get to kill her for her sins once I get all my answers. And I still plan on getting this answer from her, no matter how long it takes.

"Ten months," I say, letting her know how much time she has left, and then I end the call.

7
LIESEL

I SHOULD BE LISTENING to Waylon's speech, but all I can think about are Langston's words last night.

I've done a lot of horrible things in my life, but I have no clue which specific monstrous thing I did that Langston wants me to explain.

"With my beautiful, intelligent Liesel by my side, we will win the race for governor!" Waylon finishes his speech.

I smile brightly as he lifts my hand up, doing my part. I didn't have a speech to give today, but I will at future events.

I'm glad we've started the campaign in earnest. Waylon thinks it will stop us from being attacked with the amount of visible security he hired, but it will only slow Langston's kidnapping attempts.

Hand in hand we walk off stage, waving to the crowd and smiling so wide that my cheeks begin to hurt.

As soon as we are off stage, Waylon is swarmed by his team of people.

"I need you to look over the prenup and sign it ASAP," Nolan, his campaign manager, says to me as he thrusts some papers into my hands.

I sigh but take the papers.

Nolan is closer to my age than Waylon's. I have never seen the man not in a suit. His blonde hair swooshes over his head in a perfect wave, and his blue eyes pop with brilliance.

I haven't decided yet if I trust him or not.

"I already told you, the prenup isn't the problem," I say as I make a show of signing the damn prenup.

"You should have a big, extravagant wedding. It will bring in lots of donors and make a big splash."

"We've always discussed having a small court wedding and not making a big fuss. That way, we can show that Waylon cares about the important things. Downplay how much money he has and show that he works for the people." Also, if we have a big, splashy wedding, there is no way for me to hide it from Langston.

"Just make sure you're free three weekends from now." Nolan walks away in a huff.

I flip his back off.

I'm tired of men running my life. Waylon and I will decide when and where and how we have a wedding.

Waylon is busy talking with Nolan. I glance at the clock on my phone as I yawn. I didn't get any sleep last night.

I need some caffeine to wake me up.

I search for cafes on my phone and see a coffee shop across the street.

"Maxwell, I'm headed over to get a cup of coffee while they finish up here. You coming?" I say to the brute man in an all-black outfit. This man has nothing on Zeke, who is basically a giant, so a man like Maxwell doesn't intimidate me.

"Yes, Mrs. Brown. Wherever you go, I go."

"It's Ms. Dunn."

Maxwell frowns as he walks next to me out of the event hall.

"I'm sorry, Ms. Dunn. Nolan told me to start calling you Mrs. Brown so I wouldn't slip up when you get married, since it's happening so quickly. He said I might as well start calling you Mrs. Brown."

"I won't be changing my name even after we're married, so please call me Ms. Dunn. Or better yet, Liesel."

Maxwell stops in his tracks. "Do Mr. Brown and Nolan know about your plans? I don't think you keeping your own name will help the campaign."

"Don't worry about the campaign, Maxwell. Just worry about keeping me safe. As long as you do that, Waylon and Nolan won't have anything to complain about."

I jog across the street rather than wait at the crosswalk, forcing Maxwell to choose between almost getting hit by traffic or waiting on the sidewalk. It's a test.

He passes.

He puts his hand on the hood of a car slamming on its breaks to avoid hitting us.

I open the door to the coffee shop, and Maxwell grabs it to hold it open for me.

"No more running into danger. If I'm going to protect you, I need you to tell me your plans. I don't need you to make my job any harder than it already is."

I smirk. "That was a test. I don't usually run into danger."

His shoulders relax.

"But danger does usually find me."

And then I walk to the counter.

"Can I get a large coffee, black?"

The woman smiles at me. "That will be $3."

I hand her my credit card from my sleek white purse that pops against my navy pencil skirt and jacket.

She swipes the card a few times. "I'm sorry, but your card keeps getting declined. Do you have another one?"

I frown as I pull out another card and hand it to her. I have a sinking feeling in my stomach.

"I'm sorry, this one isn't working either."

I take the card back. I have two more cards we could try, but I suspect the same thing will happen. A line has formed behind us, and I don't have any cash.

I look to Maxwell behind me, who pulls out a ten-dollar bill and hands it to the barista.

"Keep the change," he tells her.

I walk to the other counter to wait for my drink.

"Something wrong with your card? I can tell Nolan to have the credit card company to send you a new one."

"No, that's okay. I can call myself."

Maxwell nods.

"Mind taking me to the bank?" I ask, suspecting this might be more than just a credit card issue.

"Of course."

$0.00

That's what my bank account reads.

Zero.

I haven't had an empty bank account since high school. My credit cards all have a $0 credit limit too.

I had millions saved. Millions I earned by starting my own law firm, by winning lawsuit after lawsuit.

I struggled my way through poverty, became friends with the richest boy in all of Miami, studied my ass off in college, and fought through a male-dominated world until I made my way to the top. I did all of that while wrestling with a dark past that haunts my every waking moment. I did all of that with unbearable pain. I did all of that after starting over and moving my entire life to New York.

I earned every cent, and now it's all gone.

I don't have to do any investigating to know who stole my money—Langston.

Waylon has no need for my money. I just signed the prenup. He has no right to my money any more than I have a right to his. The only money of his I can access are campaign reimbursements. We don't even plan on sharing a residence once we are married. I'll keep my apartment, and he'll keep his.

Now, I have no idea how I'm going to pay for my apartment. I can't even afford a coffee, let alone the thousands of dollars in monthly rent for my apartment.

Maxwell drives me back to my apartment as I think through my options. I refuse to rely on a man. I refuse to put myself in more debt. I won't ask Waylon for help financially. I don't even know how I'd explain to him what happened to my money in the first place.

"You okay?" Maxwell asks, raising an eyebrow in the rearview mirror as he drives.

"It was just a mixup at the bank. They recognized some fraudulent charges on my credit cards, so they canceled them. It's all sorted out now. I'm just tired."

Maxwell nods.

"Please don't mention any of this to Waylon. I don't want to worry him with something so little when he has so much going on."

I'm not sure who Maxwell is loyal to—me or Waylon. Technically, Waylon pays his salary, but I'm the one who gives Maxwell orders. Waylon made sure that Maxwell knew his job is to protect me and follow my orders no matter what. It will be an interesting test of his loyalty.

"Of course, Liesel."

He stops the car outside my building and then steps out, opening the door for me after handing the valet the keys.

I don't really need him to walk me to my door, but he won't leave me alone until I'm safely inside my apartment. I let him walk with me up into my building and up the elevator.

Once we reach my door, I expect him to come inside and search the apartment before I enter. That's what Langston would do.

"Do you need anything else, Liesel?" Maxwell stands to the side of the door as I insert the key.

I smile. "I'm good. Thanks, Max."

He grins at the nickname. "I'll be in the apartment down the hallway monitoring your door. If you need anything, just text. Otherwise, have a good night."

I walk inside and shut and lock the door behind me.

Maxwell is sweet enough. He's a decent bodyguard who I think I can trust, but he's no match for Langston or anyone who works for the Black empire.

It's an illusion of safety.

Maxwell said that he'd be monitoring the hallway, which should make it tough for me to leave without him noticing.

But he isn't the only one watching me.

I walk into the apartment, making it seem like I'm going to bed. I pull out my phone and do a quick search of surrounding hotels until I find the one Langston is staying at. It's the most expensive and closest. I know without a shadow of a doubt that he's there.

"I assume you draining my money was because you wanted to talk to me and calling me on the phone wouldn't work."

I stare up at the camera in my bedroom, talking directly to Langston.

"Meet me in the hotel bar in fifteen minutes."

I walk into the bathroom to change out of the professional-looking jacket and skirt and into something that will work to my advantage. I take my time changing into a tight black dress with lace at the hem and the neckline. I apply a dark line of eyeliner, sweep a darker shade of eyeshadow across my lids, and then pull a scarlet red lipstick out to paint my lips.

I strut out of the bathroom and fluff my hair as my eyes meet the corner of the bedroom again.

"Make me disappear," I whisper. Then I walk out of my apartment, knowing Langston will ensure that Maxwell thinks I'm still safely inside my apartment.

8
LANGSTON

IF LOOKS COULD KILL, I'd be dead right now.

Liesel struts into the hotel bar exactly fifteen minutes after speaking at me via the security camera in her apartment.

Her dress screams sex. It's black with lace and fits her like a second layer of skin. Her eyes are a darker shade than she usually wears, making her irises pop. Her red lipstick taunts me. As much as I want her lips pressed against mine, or better yet wrapped around my cock, that won't be happening. Liesel is far too pissed to let me touch her.

Even though I'm bigger, stronger, more skilled—the look in her eyes lets me know that right now, she'd win in a fight. I have to tread carefully with her.

She walks straight to the bar and sits down in the barstool next to me, her eyes never leaving mine.

"You found me. I'm impressed. I wasn't sure you still had it in you, huntress."

She growls. "I've always been the better hunter. I know you know I found you that day in your hotel room. You were hiding in the damn ceiling. The only reason I didn't climb up there and yank you out was that I came up with a better plan."

"You're welcome," I say when she finishes ranting.

She turns to face me with red eyes and flushed cheeks. "You're welcome? Are you serious? You have ruined my life more times than I can count."

I grin. *Good, I need to ruin every aspect of her life. I need every tiny thing of hers I can get my hands on before I eventually kill her. I need that to live with what she did.*

"You're welcome that I ensured Maxwell didn't see you leave. You don't have to worry about what to tell him."

She flags down the bartender with her finger. "What can I get you?" the bartender with a trimmed gray beard and piercing blue eyes asks.

"Your most expensive scotch, and put it on his tab."

He nods at her with a smile and then goes to make her drink.

She ordered the exact same thing I already ordered myself.

One minute later, he slides two glasses of scotch neat in front of us.

"Thank you," Liesel smiles at him as she takes her drink, purposefully letting her hand slide against his.

He winks back, and I suspect he'll leave his number with her by the end of the night.

"So, you like the older types?" I ask.

Liesel rolls her eyes and takes a drink. "I didn't come here so we can talk about the kind of men I find attractive. I came here to tell you to stop stealing from me." Her voice drops in revenge and pent up frustration. Her fingers tighten around the glass as her rage with me consumes her.

"Did I steal something?" I lean back in my chair, keeping my eyes on hers instead of letting myself explore every inch of her body. I have to have discipline. I have to focus on my mission.

"Don't play dumb. You stole every penny I had."

I purse my lips. "Oh, right. I did do that. But I wouldn't call it stealing."

"What would you call it?"

"I'd call it taking what I'm owed."

"You're a self-serving demon. What gives you the right to take anything from me?"

You have no idea just how much of a right I have to that money, huntress.

"You seemed to lack motivation. Taking days, months, years of your life from you wasn't working, so I took the one thing that every human responds to—money."

"You think by taking my money, I'll be forced to tell you the truth? I think you've forgotten everything I've gone through. How poor I used to be. How much of a survivor I am. I built everything I have from nothing, and I can do it again."

"Or you can marry that rich fiancé of yours."

"Husband," she says firmly.

I pull out my phone and open my browser to the announcement before sliding the phone on the oak counter in front of her.

"Liar," I whisper, cutting through the noisy bar with the single word.

Liesel freezes as she realizes she's caught in a lie.

"That little liar," she says.

"That would be you."

She slides the phone back across the bar, her frustration apparent.

My reflexes kick in, and I catch my phone before it slides off the bar.

She's glaring at the phone, not at me. I'm completely lost.

"Who's the liar?" I ask.

"No one."

"The correct answer is you—you're the liar."

"Fine, I lied, but so did you."

"I'm not the one caught in a lie. And I'm not the one who has to tell the truth in order to live—that would be you."

"Just kill me and get it over with. I'm tired of your damn games. Nothing you do will make me tell you the truth. I will go to my grave hiding my half of the letter."

"Well, you have six months left to decide."

"Six months? You took off four months for one little lie?"

"One big lie."

She downs the rest of her drink, and that's when I know that I'm getting to her. It bothers her that I'm willing to kill her.

"Whatever," she says. She pulls her own phone out and starts scrolling through news articles about her engagement announcement in frustration. It's then that I realize she hadn't agreed to the announcement. Waylon did this without her consent.

I suspected all along that Waylon isn't a good person. There is something he's hiding. I don't know what it is, but I'll figure it out long before Liesel does. I may want her dead, but I want to be the one to inflict pain. I don't want Waylon to beat me to it.

"I wouldn't trust Waylon if I were you."

"I trust him more than I trust you."

"He didn't even have your agreement before announcing your engagement. Sounds pretty untrustworthy to me."

"At least he hasn't threatened to kill me. He doesn't try to control me, unlike you."

I lean in close, getting a whiff of her sweet perfume. It's intoxicating, but I won't let it affect me.

"But does he love you?"

Her eyes narrow, her pulse races, her body stills. "He loves me more than you will ever love anyone."

"Maybe so, but I wouldn't call that love. He's just as controlling as I am. He announced your wedding without you. He made you sign a prenup. And you can't even tell him about me. It doesn't sound like true love to me."

"The announcement wasn't him—it was Nolan, his campaign manager. I had just as much money to lose as him. I don't want a man to take care of me. I want to take care of my own damn self. And not telling Waylon about you is to protect him, not because I can't.

"Waylon and I may not be head over heels in love, but our union will outlive the best marriages because we know what we are getting into. Our marriage doesn't rely on falling in and out of love. Our marriage relies on mutual respect and understanding."

I chuckle. "You don't even know who Waylon is."

Now it's her turn to lean toward me.

I hold still and try not to breathe, so I don't inhale her scent again. I can't help myself anymore, though, so I take a deep, unsettling breath.

"I know exactly who Waylon is. Just like I know who you are. I'll take my chances with Waylon."

"You don't have a clue who I am anymore. You haven't cared about my life in years."

"I know you. You're a liar, just like me."

I grin and feel her eyes on my dimples that drive her mad. "You don't have any proof of my lies, do you? You have no idea if I'm married with kids or not."

She smirks and moves her hand to mine, until she's stroking the inside of my wrist. Her eyes tilt down to my crotch.

"I don't know if you are legally married or not. I don't know if you've sired a string of bastards that are genetically related to you. What I do know is that you want me. One touch and your cock is as hard as steel. One kiss and I'm all you can think about. It doesn't matter if you're lying or not —you want me."

I remove my hand from her grasp. "I want you dead."

Her eyes dart back and forth. "I'm pretty sure that's a lie too."

"Pretty sure? That's a weak statement to bet your life on."

She stands. "My entire life has been a series of bets on my life. Somehow I've survived them all. I can survive you."

"Maybe. But right now, you have a lot less money to fight me with unless you plan on asking Waylon for help."

"I won't be asking any man for help. I've built a small empire before. My only mistake was not ensuring it was better guarded. I won't let that happen again."

"Tomorrow, I want answers. Real answers, not lies, or I'll steal more from you until you have nothing left."

She whips her hair over her shoulder. "I guess I'll just have to steal right back from you. I hope you aren't lying. I hope you are really married with kids. Because I will destroy them all. If you have a heart to break, I'll shatter it. This is war, killer."

She pauses. "And unlike you, I won't wait six months to kill you. The first chance I get, you're a dead man."

I smile. "You can't kill me, and you don't have any money to hire someone skilled enough to lay a finger on me."

Her smile is bigger than mine, which scares me. "I'll have more money than you can imagine soon enough."

With those parting words, she leaves.

Not five seconds after she leaves, I see a man I didn't expect to see here—Maxwell.

I frown; maybe he's more skilled than I thought.

9
LIESEL

I HAVE A PLAN.

Langston declared war. He has no idea why I'm with Waylon. He has no clue about all of the struggles I've been through to get the money he so easily stole from my bank account. He has no idea what I will do to continue to survive.

Six months—that was the death sentence Langston gave me. I don't give a damn about the time. Not anymore. But I do care about finding the truth.

Langston just sparked a fire in me.

This is war.

That was his goal in taking all of my money. He wanted to make me desperate. He wanted to make me beg him or Waylon for help. Dependent—that's the one thing I vowed I'd never be again. I'll do anything to protect myself before letting a man take care of me again.

Now, I want the truth, too. I want every damn secret Langston is keeping from me, and I want to use every single word against him. I want to drown him in his lies. I want to tear apart his family, his life.

I want everything from him.

But most of all—I want to know why Langston hates me. Why he started this war. *Why?*

I'm missing a crucial piece of the puzzle, and I'm tired of being left in the dark.

I'm a powerful woman. All the shit I've been through has made me invincible to pain. I no longer have fear. I no longer cry. That makes me stronger than Langston's weak ass.

He still cries. He can still feel pain. I'm stronger than him.

I have a plan.

First, I need an unlimited source of money.

Then, I'll lay my trap.

I know exactly where I'm getting the money. Thank god I signed the prenup already.

"Good morning," Waylon says as he enters my kitchen in his suit, already dressed to head into the office.

"Good morning," I say as I hold my cup of coffee and stand at the counter.

Waylon comes over and kisses me softly on the cheek. Then he heads to the coffee pot and pours himself a cup in a travel mug.

"What do you have planned for today? Headed into the office?" he asks as he secures his coffee lid.

"No, the office is running smoothly, but I thought I'd get away for the weekend."

Waylon freezes. He knows what that's code for. We have an agreement, he and I. I have needs he can't satisfy and vice versa.

He can fuck whoever he wants. I can do whatever I want. We live separate lives when we need to. Our future marriage is about mutual gain. It's about helping each other with our careers, our image, our lives. And it's about having a steady fuck in each other's bed. It's not real love, but it works for us.

It's a modern relationship that doesn't hide the fact that one single person can't possibly fulfill every single one of our needs.

It's been a while since I tested the arrangement, though. Before, it was just a verbal agreement. Now that we are getting married—it's a legal contract in our prenup.

"You'll take Maxwell with you. That isn't an option."

I nod. "I agreed to security. You should have the guys over this weekend to keep you company while I'm away." That's my way of saying he should invite a whore over to fuck since I won't be here.

Waylon walks over to me and tucks a strand of hair behind my ear. "Now that I'm running for governor, I shouldn't be seen doing such things."

His eyes bore into mine, letting me know that if I get caught, there will be consequences.

"Understood." I nod back.

"You have to tell Nolan, though." He steps back, leaning against the counter across from me.

"No way, you hired him. I'm not telling Nolan."

"He's my campaign manager. He needs to know your whereabouts in order to protect the campaign from any misunderstandings that may happen."

I glare at Waylon. "I signed an agreement with you. There is nothing in it that says I have to be the one to arrange things with your employee. You deal with him."

Waylon grins. "There is the woman I love. You know how much I enjoy your fiery spirit."

"I'll see you Monday. Take me out to dinner before the campaign event on Tuesday."

"I have the perfect place."

We exchange words back and forth with our eyes. Promises. Threats. Arrangements.

Our entire conversation is in code. Langston won't know

what we are talking about. And he definitely won't know what we aren't saying with our eyes and bodies.

But we know.

I nod.

Then, Waylon comes over and kisses me on my forehead. "I look forward to our dinner."

I swallow hard, before forcing my body to breathe.

I'm doing this to keep control, to earn unlimited amounts of money. Waylon may not be perfect, but he's not the devil. That label belongs to Langston.

There is a knock at the door. Waylon heads to the door and answers it.

"Come in, Maxwell. Liesel is almost ready. It seems you will be headed on a nice weekend trip."

"Yes, sir."

"And let me remind you if anything happens to Liesel or if her identity gets out, it will be you whom I take my wrath out on."

"Understood, Mr. Brown."

Waylon looks back and winks at me before he heads out to work.

"Where are we going?" Maxwell asks me as he enters my kitchen.

"Straight to hell."

I pull my silver mask down over my face as Maxwell parks the car in front of Pier 40 at Hudson River Park.

"You sure about this, Liesel?" Maxwell asks with uncertainty in his voice.

I take a deep breath as I stare at the yacht tied to the pier. I hate the damn ocean. It reminds me too much of my past.

Langston will always have the advantage on the water, but this weekend is about earning back power. And the only way to truly have power is with money. Once I have money, I'll be back on equal footing with Langston.

"Yes," I answer, stepping out of the car.

Maxwell steps out as well with his own mask on. He's in a tux, and a black mask covers his sculpted face, but it doesn't make him any less intimidating. He extends his arm to me, so we look like a couple as we walk up the ramp to the yacht.

I'm wearing a long dark wig to cover my blonde. That, combined with the mask and my bare ring finger, will mean no one will have a clue who I am here. That is unless Langston decides to make an appearance. I could wear a full prosthetic, don a wig, disguise my voice, and he'd still know it was me. Our connection is too intense for him to not recognize when I'm in the same city, let alone the same yacht as him.

"Nervous?" Maxwell asks as we walk up the ramp.

I nod. I'm nervous, but not for the reasons Maxwell thinks. I'm not nervous about what I plan on doing tonight or about getting caught. I'm nervous to see Langston tonight and what that could possibly mean.

"Don't be. My only job is to protect you and your identity. I'll keep you safe. You don't have to worry about that. I won't let any man hurt you or even lay a finger on you unless you want them to."

"Thank you," I say with a weak smile. I truly think Maxwell might be the only good person in all of this, but he's no match for Langston. If Langston wants to hurt me, Maxwell won't be able to stop him.

"I could protect you better if you told me your plan," Maxwell says.

My smile drops. "Sorry, Max, but I have to keep my intentions to myself."

"But Mr. Brown knows?"

My eyes cut to Maxwell as we reach the top of the ramp.

"Miss…?" A man on the yacht with a tablet asks as I approach.

"Ms. Juliane White," I say, giving a fake name.

"It's a pleasure to meet you, Ms. White. And you are?" The man turns to Maxwell.

"Mr. Maxwell," he gives me a confused glance out of the corner of his eye but goes with the flow. He doesn't know what tonight is about or what kind of yacht we just boarded. He doesn't know that he's going to have to earn his keep this weekend when some of the most powerful and dangerous men on the planet will all be gathered on this yacht.

The man nods at me. "I'll escort you to your rooms. Play starts at midnight."

I bat my eyelashes at him. "I can't wait."

The man leads me and Maxwell to two adjoining rooms, complete with a balcony and jacuzzi tub.

"You'll find everything you need inside. If not, dial one on the phone, and anything you need will be provided. The yacht leaves in two hours. As I said, play starts at midnight." Then the gentleman, who never gave us a name, leaves.

Maxwell stands frozen with his hands in his pocket, staring at me in disbelief.

"Liesel, what the heck have you gotten us into?"

I remove my mask, knowing that it will be one of the few times this weekend that I can. "Not us—me."

"I'm on the damn ship, same as you. You just gave a fake name while boarding a ship without any luggage for a weekend. What the hell is going on?"

"I pay you to follow orders, Max, not to question my decisions."

"Liesel, I'm speaking as a friend. What is going on?"

"Something was stolen from me. I'm just ensuring I get it back and that nothing else is ever stolen from me again."

10
LANGSTON

I STAND ON THE PIER, looking up at the giant yacht. Never have I been so hesitant to set foot on a boat.

Liesel came here because she needs money. Apparently, she thinks boarding this boat will help, but I've never found less information about an organization before stepping foot on their yacht than this one.

I scoured the internet but found nothing on this group. I don't even know who owns this boat, or who runs whatever excursion we are about to embark on.

My guess is this is an exclusive poker tournament or betting ring. Liesel thinks this is the fastest way to earn a lot of money since she won't ask her fiancé for money.

Their conversation the other morning was quite intriguing. So much unspoken in between them. I don't understand why they are together—*love, lust, power? What draws them together?* It can't be love. At least from Liesel's side, the woman is incapable of the emotion.

"You sure about this, boss?" Enzo asks, standing next to me in a tux and black mask—the only requirements listed to board the yacht.

"I'm not the boss. That would be your wife," I say.

Enzo shakes his head with his hands in his pockets. "We've all taken turns being in charge. This is your mission—we are here to support you. That means you're the boss, and you have to take responsibility for your actions and any lives lost."

I swallow down the acid creeping up in my throat. Almost everyone I love is standing behind me, waiting to get on this yacht if I give the order.

Kai, Enzo, Zeke, Siren, and Beckett. The only one missing is Nora, but she's watching the kids. Phoenix also stayed home to watch our kids. If I send us into a trap, five little kids could lose their parents. Nora could lose the man she loves. Phoenix could lose me.

It's a big decision to make when I don't have all the facts, but we know yachts more than we know anything. Once on board, we'll hack into the security system and figure out just what the hell is going on. And we have a crew nearby on one of our own yachts prepared to follow this one. We'll be safe—safe as we can be, anyway.

"I'm sure," I say and step forward onto the boat's boarding ramp. I hear footsteps behind me, and I don't have to glance back to know that my entire team is following me. I'm not used to being the leader or worrying about anyone except myself, but I vow to keep every one of them safe. No one gets hurt on my watch.

"Name?" a man at the top of the ramp with an iPad asks.

I could give a fake name, but my name, and the name of everyone behind me, is feared. Our names help to protect us. We won't hide.

"Langston Pearce," I say.

The man nods and gestures to a woman beside him. "Kala will see you to your room."

I start to follow the woman as the man asks Enzo his name. She leads me downstairs and through multiple hallways.

"Here is your room for this evening," the woman finally says, opening the door to a room for me before handing me the keycard.

I step inside the plain room and examine its simple bed and connected bathroom.

"Play starts at midnight," the woman says, and then she shuts the door without explaining anything else.

Play? I guess this is some type of high roller poker tournament.

I scan the room, looking for any clues. After going through every cabinet and drawer, I find nothing.

I pick up the phone.

"Do you need anything delivered to your room, Mr. Pearce? Food? Drink?" a man starts speaking as I pick it up.

"No, I'm good."

I hang up.

Hmmm.

I pull out my phone to try and hack into their system. We weren't allowed any bags, so there was no real way to sneak a laptop onto the yacht.

After scanning the room, the hallway, and the deck outside, I realize there is no system to hack into. There are no security cameras.

Strange.

I suspect there are plenty of rich people here that will need to feel protected and safe. *Why are there no cameras?*

Three quick knocks at the door.

I walk over and open it. Enzo spills into my small bedroom, followed by everyone else—Kai, Zeke, Siren, and Beckett.

"There are no cameras, are there?" Enzo asks.

"No, only the control systems in the wheelhouse to drive the yacht. There is nothing else to hack," I answer.

"So, what's the plan?" Kai asks, stepping in front of the sliding glass door to look out at the night sky.

"We keep Liesel from getting money. She's desperate. I need her that way to end this."

Kai and Siren exchange glances.

Beckett nods in agreement—I've always liked him.

Zeke shows no emotion. He's always ready to do what I ask; no questions asked—even after everything that has happened between us.

Enzo studies Siren, like he's begging her to be the voice of reason.

"No kidnapping or hurting her to get what you want. There are five of us. We can stop her from getting money or harming us without hurting her. Liesel's on our side. We just have to remind her of that," Siren says, her look threatening death if I disobey her.

Siren's wrong—Liesel isn't on our side. I don't think she was ever on anyone's side except her own.

"Promise me, no hurting or kidnapping Liesel. We've all betrayed this family at one point or another to protect ourselves or someone we love. That's all Liesel is doing. Just remind her that we all love her and want her to join us again," Siren continues as she walks to me.

I frown as she puts her hands on either side of my face. "Promise me."

There is no getting around this. Siren won't stop until I promise. And she knows I won't break a promise—not with her. I won't risk my relationship with her. Our connection is too strong. I need Siren in my life.

"I promise I won't kidnap or hurt Liesel unless she's

trying to hurt or kill one of us. I will protect everyone in this room above everything. But if Liesel tries to hurt one of you, I will stop her with whatever means necessary."

"Liesel won't try to hurt us," Siren says.

Everyone else in the room exchanges glances. Liesel has already hurt the rest of us. Siren just hasn't felt the same level of pain because she knows Liesel the least.

"She might," Kai says.

Siren's head whips to her. "You're not helping."

"I'm just being honest. Liesel is always welcome in this group, but only if she chooses to put our family first. She's not doing that right now. We don't know what she's gotten into. We don't know how dangerous she is," Kai answers.

I pull Siren to me, holding her tight against my chest to try and reassure her. "I promise I won't hurt her unless I have to."

She nods, and a soft sigh escapes her lips.

I'll do my best to keep my promise to her, at least while we are on this yacht. But someday, I'll be forced to break my promise. There is no way this ends without Liesel dead. She's done too much.

At midnight, we all leave my room and head to the center of the yacht. We are all wearing tuxes, fancy dresses, and masks to cover our faces. Although, we don't really need to hide who we are.

We are greeted by one of the employees as we walk down the hallway.

"If you could head to the top deck, you will be given more instructions from there," a man in a sharp suit says.

Wordlessly, we climb to the top deck, where several

people are already gathered. There is a small bar set up with drinks. We all walk over to get one to hold in our hands, not because any of us will be partaking. We need to be completely clear-headed for whatever we have gotten ourselves into.

"Where is she?" Zeke asks, holding a whiskey drink in his hand as he scans the deck. Everyone is dressed like this is the most extravagant party they have ever attended. And everyone has a mask on. Even so, I can spot some politicians, athletes, and models in the crowd.

"I don't see her yet," I answer.

"She better be here. I don't know what we've gotten ourselves into, but I don't like it," Zeke says.

"She will be," I say.

I tracked her phone here. She's here.

I take a sip of my scotch. I guess I'm going to be needing a bit of alcohol to get through tonight after all.

"Jesus," Zeke mumbles under his breath.

I turn to follow his gaze as chills creep up on my arms.

At first, all I see is a glimmer as her dress sparkles under the moonlight. Then my entire body adapts to Liesel being in the same space as me. She dominates everything—my attention, my breath, my heartbeat, it's all hers.

I've never seen a more sexy woman. Liesel may not care for makeup and dresses and all the foo-fooey things some girls like, but damn does she know how to wear it well. The dress is the perfect mix of skin, silk, and lace. I can see the outline of her body through the thin material—her nipples are already hard.

I finally force my eyes off her body to her face. She's wearing a glittery mask, like everyone else here. The shine of the mask makes it difficult to get a good glimpse of her eyes. That, combined with the jet black wig she's wearing, would make her almost unrecognizable to anyone else who knows her.

But she could be wearing a head to toe Mickey Mouse costume and I'd still know it was her underneath. She can't hide from me.

"Wait, I thought Kai was wearing a green dress, and what is she doing with that guy?" Zeke asks.

I snort. "That's not Kai, that's Liesel."

"Wow, she looks deadly," Zeke says.

My lips thin. "You have no idea."

I turn my attention to the man at her side—Maxwell. He's dressed like us in a sharp suit that shows off how many muscles he has beneath his jacket, and a plain black mask covers half his face. His jaw is tight, his lips showing no emotion, and his eyes scanning everyone in the room. He seems as unsettled as I feel.

It hits me all at once that he doesn't know why we're here any more than I do. I know it's about Liesel getting money to fight me, but I don't know this game we will be playing.

"Ladies and gentlemen, thank you all for coming," a man in a suit says. He's the only one not wearing a mask as he makes his way to the center of the deck.

The stars are sparkling overhead, making it feel like this is meant to be a romantic night with some rich fuckers. But I have a feeling that's part of the lure, to get us to relax and let our guard down before this game starts.

"Does everyone have a drink?" he asks, scanning the crowd of people.

Most people are nodding their heads, yes. For the few that don't have drinks, bartenders are quickly bringing around glasses to fill their hands.

Once the man in the center is assured that everyone has a drink, he continues.

"My name is Mr. Reyes. I'm here to oversee this weekend's games. I recognize a couple of familiar faces, but for the majority of you, this is your first time. I want to assure you that you will be well taken care of for as long as your stay lasts."

Enzo gives me a tight glare as we both try to figure out what's happening.

"The game is simple. The last one remaining wins the twenty million-dollar prize."

Fuck—Liesel could do a lot with twenty million. No wonder we are here. She would instantly regain everything I took from her in one weekend if she won.

"As you know, there is no buy-in. No money is required to enter. The winnings are generously provided by the ship's owner. The owner enjoys watching people get pushed to their limits. The owner and a very select group of people are the only ones watching the games along with the game's remaining participants."

So someone is watching, which means there are cameras. I just need to find them.

"What is the game exactly? I'm sure you're all eager to know."

Yes, spill, old man.

"The game is simple. Each round, you will be drawing names to be paired with. Sometimes it will be a one on one competition. Other rounds might be a group of four competing. The goal is to push your competitor to their sexual limits until they withdraw from the competition."

Fuck.

My eyes find Liesel. She's standing casually in the same spot she was before. Her heart isn't thumping wildly, her lips are relaxed, and she takes a quick sip of champagne.

I frown. She knew exactly what she was walking into and did it anyway. These are sex games. Liesel can't give up control when it comes to sex, so I don't know how she expects to win.

"The game lasts two days. Most of you won't make it past tonight's rounds. You can withdraw at any time for any reason. But if you withdraw tonight, you will be leaving us. You will not get to stay to watch tomorrow's events. If you make it to tomorrow, even if you withdraw, you can remain and watch the final rounds if you so choose."

Everyone is eerily silent as Mr. Reyes speaks. There are a few people who seem unfazed—the ones who have been here before. Others are licking their lips in anticipation of what is about to happen. And still, others are jittery, shifting their weight in the spot where they stand or tapping their fingers or heels to try and get the nervous energy out.

I don't have to glance at my family to know that they will all end up withdrawing by the end of the night unless they draw the names of their spouses. None of them are prudes, but I can't imagine Enzo sitting by watching Kai getting fucked by some stranger here. Nor Zeke watching Siren. Nora may not be here, but I suspect Beckett won't push things too far if he wants a chance with her. That means it'll be up to me to remain in the game.

"What about security?" Maxwell asks.

"I assure you this yacht is completely secure, and my team is here to ensure no one gets hurt who doesn't want to. You will be pushed to your limits if you remain in the game, but you will have a safe word to use at any time that will alert my team to get you out of here quickly and safely.

"Everyone here must participate in the game or go home. We don't allow bystanders to just watch or protect. If you feel that you need to remain to protect someone in the game, then you must participate and advance."

Maxwell frowns and almost kills the guy with one look.

I feel his pain. Maxwell won't last the night, but I will. Tomorrow he won't be here to protect Liesel.

"If there are no more questions, we will begin. Everyone's name and safe words are already in this bowl. I will randomly draw two names at a time to match partners for the first round. Let the games begin."

11
LIESEL

I KNEW there was a chance that Langston would be here, but seeing him standing in a suit and black mask has my heart skipping beats so often that I'm afraid I'm going to flatline and die right here right now.

It was a risk I took coming here to earn my money back. My win was almost guaranteed if I was here alone, but having Langston in the game changes everything.

I can't stop looking at him in his tux. His chiseled jaw, sharp eyes, and smooth hair would make it seem like he spends every weekend in a tux. In reality, he wears jeans and boots and kills people every day of the week. He's not comfortable in a tux, in this wealthy, extravagant world. I need to remember that and try to use it to my advantage if I can.

Beat, my reckless heart. Beat hard and steady—I'm going to need every drop of blood and ounce of oxygen in my body to flow through me if I'm going to win.

What surprises me the most is seeing the rest of the gang all here, flanking Langston like he's the leader instead of Enzo and Kai.

They had no idea what they just walked into. Their tense bodies and guarded expressions make it clear they want to be anywhere but here.

I smirk, raising my champagne glass meant to make me look girly and feminine instead of the scotch I really want. Adding them to the game will make it easier to win if I'm matched with one of them. None of them will be able to withstand watching their partner get fucked.

No, the only threat to me is Langston—for so many fucking reasons.

Maxwell leans over to whisper in my ear. "I'll try to stay in as long as I can. I promise I'll at least make it to tomorrow."

I tilt my head up at him. "Don't worry about protecting me. I can protect myself here. Stay if you want to stay, but don't do anything that will wreck your soul for my sake."

I said the wrong thing. Maxwell's face morphs into a horrified expression. He's beyond worried.

I laugh. "Just fuck some women if you want to, Max, but don't do it on my account." I pat his chest, trying to calm him, but his heart is beating wildly out of control.

He clears his throat and exhales.

Poor, Max. I doubt he lasts the first round.

A woman brings a large glass bowl out, while a man brings a small table. The table is positioned, and the woman sets the bowl down upon it.

"Round one is a partner game. I'll draw two names who will be competing against each other and the clock. There will also be your individual safe word on the paper as I draw them. Memorize this safe word. If you mutter it, you are withdrawing from the game. Your challenge will immediately stop, and you'll be escorted out. Round one will take place here on the upper deck as there is the most amount of room."

Mr. Reyes tries a comforting smile on his face as he scans the crowd.

"Let's begin." He reaches into the glass bowl and pulls out a name.

"Ms. Laine," he says the name of Laila Salo, an actress using a fake name.

She walks over and takes the card with her name on it. Her breath hitches as she waits for her partner to be drawn.

"Mr. Fray," he says.

A gentleman almost twice her age walks over to her.

Her smile falters for only a second, but she recovers before almost anyone notices. This is a game of bluffing and chicken more than anything else. Most people think they would be willing to do anything for twenty million, especially sexual things with mostly wealthy and good-looking people. When it actually comes down to it, they are dead wrong.

Mr. Reyes pulls out another card. "Mr. Pearce."

I raise an eyebrow as my eyes go to Langston's. He gave his real name. *Ballsy*. That or he thinks using his real name will intimidate people more.

My heart, my breath, and all other bodily functions stop as I wait for Langston to walk over to collect his card and wait for Mr. Reyes to announce his partner.

Anyone but me.

"Ms. Fraser."

I gasp, sucking in oxygen, trying to restart my body.

"Are you okay?" Maxwell asks me.

I nod silently as a pretty redhead approaches Langston. He gives her a tense smile, and then they move to the side as more names are called.

"Mr. Kane."

"Mrs. Kane."

Zeke and Siren smile at each other, happy to be partnered with their spouse. It will ensure they last this round, but that's it. Once they are re-partnered, they will be gone.

"Mr. Maxwell," Mr. Reyes says.

"Good luck," I whisper to him as he walks forward.

Maxwell is paired with a woman in her mid-fifties, and he doesn't hide his disgust well.

I smile behind my glass. He won't last round one.

I'll be truly on my own after this round.

"Mrs. Black."

Kai walks forward like she owns the room, the most powerful woman here.

There are whispers and gasps as she steps forward, proudly using her name and being herself.

It's all a facade, though. She won't so much as kiss another man, or let any man but Enzo fuck her.

"Mr. Ito."

A tall, handsome gentleman steps forward. He's good looking, but he glances in fear at Enzo as he walks. I wouldn't be surprised if the man simply dropped out so that he didn't have to deal with Enzo's wrath for touching his wife.

"Mr. Beckett."

"Ms. Abara."

Beckett wordlessly and expressionlessly takes his spot by his partner, who looks like she is about his age.

"Ms. White."

That would be me. I step forward and feel everyone's eyes on me as I collect my card.

I don't bother to glance at the safe word as I tuck the card into my bra. Everyone notices, and there is a collective hush around the room.

I will look at the safe word later, but I won't be needing it this round. I know my limits, and really, I only have one. This round won't be the one where that limit is crossed.

I feel Langston's stare more intensely than anyone else's. He has questions. He wants to know why I chose a fake name. He wants to know what a rape victim who has trouble fucking anyone is doing in the middle of a dangerous sex game.

Just more secrets I'll be taking to my grave.

"Mr. Black."

My eyes cut to Enzo as a smug smile crosses my lips.

Jesus, could this first-round be any easier?

Enzo walks stoically toward me as he collects his card. He, unlike me, looks at the safe word. He's going to be needing it.

We stand to the side as the rest of the names are called.

"What did you get us into, Liesel?" Enzo asks me.

"I didn't get you into anything. This is Langston's fault when he stole everything from me."

"You could have come to any of us for money, and we would have given it to you."

"But then it wouldn't have been mine. I would have owed you a debt, and I'm tired of owing men debts."

His eyes narrow as he tries to find the meaning behind my words.

"Round one is limited to thirty minutes. Enjoy your time together. Push the limits. But remember, the word 'no' has no power here. You can say no, but that doesn't mean your partner has to stop. The only word with any power to stop the madness is your safe word. Use it, and your time here ends. Keep the word from your mouth, and you'll move on to the next round, where more pleasure awaits you, but so does more pain. Round one starts now."

Round one isn't where things get interesting. There are too many people in the game that have no sense being here. People are too timid in round one. I plan on making it to the end, so I won't hold back.

I've fucked Enzo Black and been raped by his father. There is no limit too far when it comes to him. I'd love to enjoy making him bleed, but I doubt I'll get the chance to take things that far.

"So, what happens now?" Enzo asks as people around us nervously start talking, some touching or tentatively kissing.

I down the rest of my champagne, letting the sweet liquid burn my throat, and then I calmly place my glass on one of the little cocktail tables.

Enzo is still gripping his scotch glass.

I take Enzo's free hand.

"Liesel, I'll give you the money, you don't have to do this."

I kiss the palm of his hand, knowing I won't get a reaction from him. But I want to draw some blood before he calls out his safe word like the pussy he is. The only way to do that is to take my time with him.

"What? You think I'm whoring myself out to make money?"

The tick in his jaw confirms that is exactly what he thinks of me. He doesn't realize the way to win this game is to push your partner before they push you. Keep the upper hand, the control, the power, and you win. Lose it for a second, and you might as well forfeit because there is no way to come back.

My gaze finds Kai's as my teeth sink into Enzo's wrist like a vampire drawing blood.

He winces as my teeth pierce his skin, but he doesn't surrender. He's a man who can handle pain. He's lived it just like me.

He grabs me by the neck and yanks me to him. "Don't play games with me, Liesel. You'll lose. You've lost every time."

"I lost because my protectors failed me. But I don't lose when I'm protecting myself."

My hand shoots down his pants, and I squeeze, hard.

He releases my neck, and I plant a wet, passionate kiss on his lips as my hand strokes his cock.

His hands are at my shoulders in a second, and he shoves me harshly back. I stumble back in my heels, but I'm not pissed. I just won.

"Pergola," Enzo says, saying his safe word.

Two men come over to immediately escort Enzo out.

I wave at him as the men put hands on his arms to lead him out. He shakes them off, gives me a glare vowing his revenge, and then walks out on his own accord.

Kai is staring me down.

"You're welcome," I mouth, knowing that she doesn't want to watch her husband kiss another girl.

She stands frozen, not sure whether to thank me or kill me for touching her man, even if it ensured that no other woman would touch him.

Kai turns back to her partner, and they chat. The man doesn't touch her. He's too afraid of what will happen. She'll remain in this round, but eventually, she'll be partnered with a man who isn't afraid of her husband.

I glance around at the other couples.

Zeke and Siren are holding each other and whispering, most likely a plan, to each other.

Beckett has his girl on her knees, pulling his cock out and stroking him.

Interesting, he might be better at this game than I thought.

Maxwell's partner moves to undo his pants, and he calls out his safe word. He turns to look at me to apologize.

I laugh and shake my head. *I knew he wouldn't last.*

And then I see Langston. He's making out with his model partner. His hands are all over her. He's completely in control. Every time she tries to touch him, he grabs her hands and stops her. Forcing her hands behind her back, he spins her around and kisses down her neck.

She seems to be enjoying herself. But then he whispers something into her ear, and her face turns white.

She gulps like she can't get enough air. That's when I realize he's gripping her neck, too. She can't breathe.

I frown. This is one of the many reasons I don't want Langston in the game. He's smart and controlling and sexy—all weapons in this game.

Men have an advantage in the initial rounds because of their strength. Like Langston is doing now, they can overpower a woman to win.

But women have an advantage in the later rounds when that strength is taken away. With restraints, it becomes about limits. If you can read your partner and identify their weakness, that's when you have the advantage. Knowing if they can handle pain themselves or if they'd rather be the one inflicting it.

Langston releases the woman's neck as he kisses her so tenderly. He smirks at me, knowing I'm watching him. Half of the room is watching him. Neither of them is undressed compared to the majority of the room. Some brave souls are already fucking their partners. But Langston demands attention. He sucks in all the air around us, drawing us all to see what he will do next.

He raises her dress until her ass is visible. He slaps it hard, hard enough that water stings her eyes. Her mascara starts to run down her cheeks.

Langston fists her hair as he whispers something else into her ear.

She sucks back the tears.

He's playing with her, like this is a random Tuesday. This is ordinary for him.

He slaps her ass again, and this time she calls out his

name loudly. So loudly that the few people that were fucking and not paying attention stop and turn to watch them too.

This woman could be a submissive, someone who craves pain, and it wouldn't matter. She would still lose. At this point, all Langston has to do is tell her to say her safe word, and she will. She's completely under his control.

Langston notices the attention he's getting. It's a power move so that whoever he's partnered with next knows to desire and fear him in the same breath. And yet, I think the only reason he's putting on a show is because of me. He wants me to know that he won't play around. That married or not, he's in this game, same as me—to win.

I drag my eyes away, forcing myself to look out at the ocean instead of him. I hear another slap, and I can feel his hand on my own skin. My fingers trace over my collarbone, trying to distract myself, but it's a useless endeavor. Whenever we're in the same room, all I feel is him.

Now that he's purposefully trying to pull my attention, my entire body is screaming to touch him, to kiss him, to want him.

"One-minute warning," Mr. Reyes says.

That's when I hear the woman Langston is partnered with call out her safe word.

The room gasps as she says it, not because she's being tortured or pushed, but simply because Langston told her to.

"That's the end of round one. Congrats on making it through, but the night isn't finished yet. We will give you ten minutes to regroup before the next round begins."

I'm standing outside on a yacht in the middle of the ocean, and yet, I can't breathe. I can't get enough oxygen. Not with Langston so near and smelling like sex. I want to jump into the ocean and swim until I can't any more, but that wouldn't solve any of my problems.

Instead, I grab a glass of scotch and head to my room to

get myself off. Ten minutes isn't a long time, but I need a release if I'm going to survive the next round. I just pray I'm never partnered with Langston, because that's the only way I might lose. And I can't lose.

12
LANGSTON

"THAT'S the end of round one," Mr. Reyes says.

Thank fuck.

I'm so wound up, every nerve in my body is firing, overloading my brain. Lust, want, fear, desire, anger, pain—they all mix together.

But the one single thing that sticks out is that by the end of this game, I know my soul will be lost to the fires of hell. Not because I'm going to fuck complete strangers, or take advantage of them until they are screaming to stop. We are all adults here. No one is forcing anyone. People attend parties like this because of the excitement, the danger.

They just didn't expect a sick fucker like me to show up. One who doesn't give a damn about anyone except the blonde in a dark wig who just ran out of the room, taking my soul with her. Somehow, she stole it, and I haven't been able to get it back.

At least it's not my heart.

I have ten minutes until the next twisted round.

Enzo is out.

Maxwell is out.

By pure luck of the draw, Kai, Siren, Beckett, and Zeke remain.

Zeke flashes me a look, gesturing to come strategize with him. He's going to warn me that there is no way any of them are going to last another round. They won't stand by watching their spouses fuck a sick bastard just to try to protect me, or stop Liesel from winning.

I don't want to spend my ten minutes talking to them. I already know they can't help.

Instead, I chase after the woman who is always running from me. The woman who has my soul locked in a cage somewhere deep in her body and set it on fire. Together we burn. Neither of us will survive like this, but I have to survive.

I have to free my soul and every other part of me she's tried to claim.

I run downstairs and look left then right when I get to the hallway of bedrooms.

Which way did she go?

Right.

I walk down the hallway, listening carefully like I'm going to be able to hear her heart beating through the thick doors.

I might if it's beating anywhere as loudly as mine.

That was intense. Not the woman I had my way with—she was nothing. But Liesel's eyes on me—being able to feel her from across the room, I've never felt anything like it.

And I'm not sure I can win if we don't break the connection now.

I try knocking on several doors, but I get no answer. Either she's not in these rooms, or she's not opening the door to me.

I get to the end of the hallway, and I know before I knock that this is her room.

Gently, I let my knuckles tap against the door and hopefully rattle her.

There is a hiss of breath coming from the other side, as if she just got burned. *I know the feeling, baby.*

A minute later, Liesel opens the door.

She tugs on her dress, trying to straighten it out. Her cheeks are pink beneath the glittery mask, her eyes wild.

I glance past her, almost expecting a man to be in the room. There is no one else.

I take a deep breath and then smirk.

"What are you doing here?" she asks.

"I turned you on so much that you couldn't even wait ten minutes for your next partner to get you off. You had to do it yourself?"

Her cheeks turn a bright shade of red, but her eyes tighten to slits trying to break through my skin with her gaze.

"No."

I grab her hand and lift it to my nose. "Liar, I can smell your cum on your fingers."

She yanks her hand away. "Just trying to satisfy myself since I know no man here will. It helps me keep a level head during play."

"You've been here before, haven't you?"

She doesn't answer my question. "I guess asking you if you're married is a moot point. If you are, it's only on paper. No man would touch a woman like that if he were in love or even getting regular sex at home."

"I guess Waylon is just a man you can use for power. Why stay with him when you can just whore yourself out for money?"

She slaps me.

I could have stopped her, but I like her all worked up and

angry. It will make it harder for her to win if she can only concentrate on me and nothing else.

"Quit now, Langston. You and all of your friends need to use your safe word and get out of here. This isn't a good place to be. Tonight is nothing. Tomorrow..." she lets her voice drop as she brushes past me.

I let her because our time is up; we both need to get back to the top deck if we are going to be on time. Something about the way she spoke has me on edge. It's more than her just wanting to win the money to get back on equal footing. There is something I'm missing.

Liesel has definitely attended these games before. *Did she win? What the hell happened to her? Why does she look like she's seen a ghost? And why does it feel like she'd be here even if I hadn't stolen all her money?*

I jog after her and make it to the top deck just as Mr. Reyes starts up the next round.

"Ms. White, Mr. Kane, and Mr. Young. You three will form the first group."

Liesel, Zeke, and a man who looks twenty all stand together to the left of Mr. Reyes.

He continues to draw names. Apparently, we are forming groups of three this time. I must have missed the first set of instructions.

"Mrs. Kane, Mr. Pearce, and Mr. Lloyd will be the next group."

I groan as I walk over to Siren and a middle-aged man.

"Mr. Beckett, Mrs. Black, and Mr. Cole."

A couple more rounds of names are given.

"You have one hour together. Enjoy yourselves. Test your limits. Remember the reward at the end if you win. This will be the final round of the night. Whoever makes it through this round will make it to tomorrow, where everything will change. Begin."

I glance around at the two other groups I care about. Beckett, Kai, and a random man. Kai will lose, but Beckett will protect her for as long as he can.

Then, I find Liesel. She's paired with Zeke and another man who is almost as big and tall. The two men could gang up on her. They could tear her apart, rip her to shreds. Bruise her, gag her, hurt her. It's two against one. I don't like her odds. The only thing working in my favor is that Zeke won't want to do anything sexual to Liesel. But he'll have no problem holding her down while the other man fucks every one of her holes and suffocates her to within an inch of her life.

"Zeke won't hurt her," Siren whispers to me.

I grunt. "He's hated her since we were kids. He'll enjoy hurting her."

"That was before he knew you were in love with her."

I laugh. "I'm not in love with her."

"Then why else are you going through all this trouble? I know you say for the treasure, but that's just stupid. Why?"

"Maybe it's because I hate her, and this is the best way to make her pay."

"We only have an hour. Are we going to get started, or you two going to waste everyone's time? Because I have no problem using my shirt as a gag if it will shut you two up," Mr. Lloyd says.

I size the man up. He's tall and lanky. Built like a swimmer's body. He has muscles, and he's fit, but he doesn't have the bulk strength that I do. I also doubt he has the intelligence. That's not me just being cocky; I'm smarter than almost everyone else I know.

"If you're so impatient, then you start. But if you go anywhere near my asshole, I'll punch you until your lights are out. Got it?" I say.

He chuckles. "You aren't going to make it long if you can't handle some anal play from another guy. First time?"

I don't answer. I don't have a problem fucking anyone—woman, man makes no difference. Sex is just that—sex.

But I don't like anyone else taking control. Liesel and I have that same problem.

I looked at Liesel less than a minute ago, and yet, I'm already finding her again. Just as I suspected, Zeke has Liesel's arms tied behind her back while Mr. scumbag is running his hands up and down her body.

I growl. *No one touches what is mine.*

I want to run over and stop the man from touching her. She doesn't want this. There is no possible way she'd ever let a strange man touch her. She does the touching, the kissing, the fucking. She didn't even let Waylon, her fiancé, take control during sex. He was her submissive puppy.

I'm about to break all the rules and go over and put a stop to this when Liesel glances my way. There is a twinkle of mischief in her eyes, and I realize she's completely in control. I don't know what her plan is, but it's there.

That twinkle immediately disappears as soon as Siren puts her hands around me from behind and begins unbuttoning my shirt.

"What are you doing?" I hiss.

"Making Liesel jealous. Her look says she suspects we're going to breeze through this round because she already thinks you and I have fucked."

I curse.

Siren kisses my neck like we are lovers, like she's already intimately acquainted with every area of my body.

"Zeke isn't going to like it," I whisper back as Mr. Lloyd starts walking over to join in on the fun.

"Let me worry about Zeke. Just keep me away from Lloyd."

I roll my eyes. "You're going to owe me."

Siren whips me around, grabbing onto my tie. "No, you're going to owe me."

I won't be able to hold off Mr. Lloyd forever, and I can't fuck Siren. I can't take things that far. Zeke would have my balls and my head. He probably will no matter what. But I sure as hell can make Liesel think that there is something between Siren and me. I can make her fucking insane; then, I might be able to get some answers tonight.

I slip my jacket off and toss it at Mr. Lloyd.

"I'm not your coat rack," he growls, tossing my jacket to the floor.

"Let me have my way with her first. Then you can have a turn before we take her together."

"I'd rather fuck your tight ass," he smirks back.

"Fine," I hiss. "Just give me ten minutes with her first."

Mr. Lloyd grins. "I'm going to enjoy the show."

Siren raises an eyebrow in surprise. I frown in return.

Really? You think I'd ever let him fuck me?

Siren laughs. "This is going to be fun."

"Not when Zeke hangs me by my balls later." I grab Siren's curvy hips and yank her to me hard, taking her breath away.

"I enjoy a jealous Zeke. He fucks me so much harder when he's angry."

I grab her hair and yank her head back, exposing the skin on her long neck. "Can you not talk about you and Zeke fucking? I don't really want to know that I'm turning you on." I let my tongue lap down her neck, like a dog thirsting for water. Tasting Siren like this does nothing. She's a beautiful woman, but I think of her as a sister. She's my best friend. My soulmate. My partner in crime. She's not my lover.

"Eww," Siren says but the way she says it makes anyone

looking on think I just made her come with my tongue on her neck alone.

Her hands go to my shirt, and she continues to unbutton it as her lips kiss my chest. "Are they watching?"

I can feel Liesel's heated gaze. "Yes."

I let my eyes cut to them, and I about fucking lose it.

Liesel's dress has been ripped from her body. Zeke is using the remnants of her dress to tie her arms together, while the other guy slobbers on her neck.

"We need to up our game," I tell Siren.

Her eyes cut to them. "He won't hurt her."

"He will if he thinks I'm fucking you."

Siren yanks off my shirt and then goes to work on my belt. I face them as I shove Siren down on her knees in front of me. I won't strip her of her clothes, but I sure as hell am going to let her go further than I ever thought I would.

This isn't chicken between me and Siren. It's chicken between me and Zeke.

I look at Liesel, who is cringing with each kiss, biting her lip in disgust.

"You want Zeke to hurt Liesel?" Siren asks when she has my pants undone. I know what she's asking. *How far do I want her to go?* She's willing. She'd do almost anything for me after everything I've done for her.

I want Zeke out of the games. I want a more fair match between Liesel and the other man. She has no chance as long as he's holding her back and letting the other man do whatever he wants to her.

"Yes," I blow out.

In that second, she has my cock out, and her lips are wrapping around it.

"Jesus," I curse too loud.

I was expecting her to pull my cock out, and maybe fake touch me. I wasn't expecting a fucking blowjob.

Slap.

Zeke slaps Liesel so fucking hard across the cheek. All I see is red. Sure, my cock is hard, but there are a million naked hot people around me all moaning. Liesel is standing basically naked in front of me. Of course, I'm turned on.

You're a deadman, I mouth to Zeke. How dare he touch my woman.

Without thinking, I grab Siren's hair and fist it in a ponytail. Then I pump her head back and forth over my cock.

I'm numb. I don't feel her warm lips, wet tongue, moist saliva. All I see is Zeke's hand across Liesel's face.

Surrender, asshole. Or I'm going to take this too far.

Zeke screams pineapple.

What?

It's then that I realize it's his safe word.

I release Siren.

She removes my cock from her mouth and whispers her word.

Even as quietly as she whispered it, a man walks over to escort her out with Zeke.

"I'm sorry," I whisper to her as she stands on her feet.

"I'm not. Zeke's going to fuck me so hot tonight." She winks, and then she's led out behind Zeke.

I glance over to Liesel, who now has the man she's with tied up and on his knees.

Thanks for your help, she mouths in my direction.

"You're a sucker. I don't know who that woman is to you, but you just fell into her trap. She couldn't manipulate two men, so she had you get rid of one for her," Mr. Lloyd says behind me.

I know he's right.

"Now, about that asshole," he continues.

Like hell, I'm going to let anyone near my ass right now.

I turn and grab Lloyd by the neck.

"Ooh, you're into erotic asphyxiation? Me too," he says.

"Soon, you won't be."

I squeeze hard around his neck as I shove him toward the railing. He'll either die from lack of oxygen, or I'll throw him overboard. Either way is a win-win for me.

I lean in close to him, so no one can see that nothing sexual is happening between us. In the darkness, it looks like we are kissing. There are no rules, but I'm guessing that whatever you are doing has to at least be perceived as sexual. If not, this would just be a fistfight to the end.

Lloyd's eyes bulge and his hands grip mine, scratching them until I release enough for him to speak.

"Ready to say your safe word yet?"

"Not fair. You have to be doing something sexual. Otherwise, I can tell the owners, and they will remove you from the games when I remove myself."

Dammit.

I force my lips over his as I squeeze around his neck again. This is actually better. I can assure he can't breathe if I've sealed his mouth and blow carbon dioxide in his face.

I don't take a breath. My mouth is locked over his. My tongue dances at the seam of his lips that feel swollen from lack of oxygen.

Finally, I release him.

He mutters a word—his safe word.

I release him and walk away.

I find Liesel. Her man has her leaning against the railing, and his head is buried between her legs, tasting every inch of her.

My mouth waters at the sight as her eyes roll back. But just as she predicted, he can't get her to completion.

Her nails dig into the poor man's back, drawing blood.

"My turn," I can hear her say.

The man's eyes light up like he's just entered heaven.

She kneels in front of him.

Don't fall for it, man. The devil lives in her eyes. I wouldn't let her near your man parts right now.

She takes his cock into her mouth in one deep swallow, and he's down her throat. It's not that impressive since the guy isn't that big to begin with.

Suddenly, she bites down.

I wince at the sight as a blood-curdling scream echoes through the ship.

A man walks over to him. "I need you to say your safe word if you want to end your games."

Liesel still has her mouth around his penis as his blood drips down her chin.

The man is still screaming hysterically, but he can't seem to remember his safe word.

"Say your safe word, and this ends," the man is basically pleading with him to use his safe word.

"I can't...remember." He stutters.

"It's pterodactyl."

"Pterodactyl!" he screams.

Liesel takes her time releasing the man. When she finally unsheathes him, two more men rush over to carry her victim away.

Liesel stands up with blood dripping down her chin and onto her bare breasts. She's completely naked, covered in the man's blood with his saliva dripping between her legs.

I grind my teeth together.

"This ends tonight's game. There are eight of you left. The games start tomorrow at midnight. Enjoy the rest of your night and day tomorrow, but make sure you get plenty of rest. Tomorrow's games last as long as it takes to crown a winner."

As soon as Mr. Reyes finishes speaking, Liesel takes off. Everyone moves aside, too scared of her to stand in her way.

I chase after her, through the hallways, down the stairs.

She's about to slam her bedroom door shut, but I catch it.

My eyes take in everything—the fucking sexiest woman I've ever seen. She looks like a vampire. I have no doubt she's more powerful right now than any vampire in any novel or movie I've ever seen. She's fucking glowing with strength.

"You should have said your safe word, killer. Tomorrow, you'll be the one I'm taking a bite out of."

I shake my head. "I would worry about tomorrow later if I were you. Tonight, we are playing my game. Tonight, I want to hear a lie. Tell me all the lies, because I can't wait another night to kill you."

13
LIESEL

He wants me to lie.

I must have really gotten under his skin. And now he's here getting under mine, taking in every ounce of my nakedness.

I still have blood on my face from biting Mr. Young. I'm sweaty and sticky from being manhandled and his failed attempts at making me come.

My hair is wild, and my makeup must be dripping from my face. The only piece of clothing I still wear is my mask.

Langston is shirtless, and the top of his pants are still undone, but he has a lot more clothes on than I do. He's sweaty, but no blood covers him. He looks almost dignified.

"We should both get some rest. Tomorrow night is going to take every ounce of strength," I say.

He forces his way inside my room, and I push the door shut behind him.

"But by all means, please come in."

He snorts as he turns to look at me with his heady eyes, hooded and dripping in lust and desire.

He's just as turned on and unsatisfied as me. That's why

he's looking at me like this. Not because he finds me attractive, I remind myself.

I want to get dressed, put a robe on at least. I feel weak without clothes on, but I can't let him know that. Tomorrow if I get to wear any articles of clothing other than my mask all night, I'll be lucky. I need to get used to it. I need to feel powerful naked.

Somehow though, being nude in front of everyone else makes me strong. But in front of this man, with his eyes dancing over my body, I feel powerless.

My memories flutter through everything that has happened tonight, but only playing the parts that included Langston. Him kissing and groping the first woman, completely in control. Siren down on her knees, pleasuring him. Him threatening his male partner.

"She really loves you, doesn't she?" I ask out of nowhere. It's the only thing I can concentrate on.

"Who? Phoenix?" Langston says sheepishly, like it's too much for him to think of Phoenix while he's living this life.

"No," I shake my head. "Siren."

There is a beat of truthful silence as Langston and I trade breaths.

"Yes. Siren loves me, and I love her."

I can feel how heavily his heart beats for her. How he'd do anything in the world for her and she him.

"What is it like? Loving someone and being loved?"

"It's the most incredible and terrifying thing in the world."

I nod.

"Don't get it twisted, though. Siren and I aren't lovers. Until tonight, we'd never touched each other and never kissed."

"I know. It's not a sexual thing between you. It's not what Siren has with Zeke. It's different, but it's still love."

Langston nods as he turns and looks out the sliding glass door behind him. I walk up beside him, and we both stare out at the stary night.

"Phoenix—" Langston starts.

"It doesn't matter if you are married to her or not. It's clear you don't love her. Not after I've seen what you loving a woman looks like. You don't have that with Phoenix as far as I've seen. And no man who truly loves his wife would be able to stomach what you did tonight. That's why Enzo and Zeke dropped out so easily." I smile, thinking about what Siren did. "Zeke is going to punish Siren for touching your cock, isn't he?"

Langston chuckles. "Probably. Siren thinks it will spice up their sex life. I, for one, don't want to think about it."

I stare at his dimple and the twinkle in his eyes. For a split moment, he's happy. He's content. He's not thinking about how to get the treasure. He's not thinking about my lies. He's not thinking about killing me. He's just living in the moment.

Langston reaches into his back pocket and pulls out his phone. After a couple of swipes, he hands it to me.

"My marriage to Phoenix is legal. It may not be a fairy tale. It may not be love, but it's real."

I stare at the photo of his marriage license. I have no reason to believe he faked this. It looks real enough, and it doesn't matter. He signed a legal document, the same way I'm going to in a couple of weeks. That doesn't mean he's in love with her.

Would it matter if he was?

I don't want Langston to ever fall in love with me. I could never fall in love with him. *Maybe if he loved another woman, it would make our relationship easier? Maybe he'd be able to focus on her instead of whatever this feud is between us?*

Slowly, Langston turns to face me. His hands touch the

bottom of my glittery mask. The mask makes me feel beautiful and mysterious, even though it doesn't hide who I really am.

He pushes the mask off my face and tosses it on the bed.

Then he tugs gently on the black wig I'm wearing.

"I don't like this," he says.

"No?"

"No."

His hands pull the wig off next. I've never felt so bare and so seen.

My blonde hair is up in a bun.

With his eyes locked on mine, he tugs the elastic, and my hair falls in waves down my neck.

"Better," he says.

We both stare at each other, breathing deeply. He said he came here for me to tell a lie so he could take more time off my life. But right now, it seems he came here to see into my soul.

"About the lie…we should talk so I can shower and sleep," I say.

He frowns and takes my hand.

"First, I need to wash the blood, sweat, and saliva from your body."

"Then?"

He smirks. "I'm going to enjoy the 'then' step the most, probably for quite a while. After we do that, you will tell me a lie to soothe my rage at this mess you got us all in."

First, he wants to wash me.

Then, he won't say.

Lastly, he wants me to tell him a lie.

I don't think I'm going to survive this night.

"Why?" I ask.

His jaw ticks. His teeth grind. Langston doesn't like to be

defied. He doesn't give orders often, but when he does, he wants them obeyed without question.

"I hold your life in the palm of my hand. If you want to survive the year, you'll do as I say."

I bite my lip. He has no idea how wrong he is.

Langston walks to the bathroom, and I follow.

Maybe I follow out of survival.

Maybe I follow out of curiosity.

Maybe I follow out of desire.

The bathroom door reveals a giant jacuzzi tub.

"They gave you a nice suite," he says.

"Yours doesn't come with a hot tub?"

He shakes his head as he flips on the water and pours some nearby bath salts into the water.

I'm already naked, and I assume the tub is just for me, so I move to climb into it, knowing the water and bit of bubbles will make me feel more covered up.

Langston holds out a hand, stopping me.

I frown.

My eyes bulge as he undoes the zipper on his slacks and pushes them down until he's naked in front of me. His cock strains in my direction.

My mouth waters, looking at the large veins on his member pointing in my direction. I've never been so jealous of Siren. She got to taste it, touch it, suck it.

My heart is beating wildly in my chest. *Does he expect me to fuck him?*

Silently, he steps into the tub. Then, he holds his hand out to me.

I take it. My brain is mush, unable to think through any decision. He could tell me to jump off the balcony into the ocean right now, and I'd probably do it.

We are standing face to face in the tub as the water fills to just below our knees. I've seen Langston shirtless before, but never naked like this. His muscles are a perfect sculpture of man. Leonardo da Vinci couldn't have sculpted a more perfect specimen. But it's offset by scars, cuts, bruises that show why he really has the muscles. It's not because he wants to look good; it's out of necessity.

I want to bask in the view of his cock again, but I'm too afraid. Not of what Langston would say but what I might accidentally do if I let myself go there. I'd be a goner.

Langston turns me around until I'm no longer facing him, and then we both sink down into the water, my back to his front.

I purse my lips, trying to breathe slowly out. I need to slow my breathing, my heart rate, everything if I'm going to have a chance of keeping my lust in check.

"Relax. I'm just washing you. I won't rape you."

I'm not sure if he touched me right now, it would be rape. I'm pretty sure my body would be begging for it, and my mind would go right along with it.

I still don't know why he's washing me, spending time with me tonight. *Trying to get under my skin? Learn secrets that will help him tomorrow?*

There is a sponge lying on the edge of the tub. Langston grabs it and wets it before he squeezes it over my head to wet my hair and face.

Once he does that, I can breathe again as the iron taste of blood begins to wash from my lips.

I can't believe I bit that guy's penis, but whatever it takes to survive. I will survive at all costs. I made that promise a long time ago. I'm just afraid I'll break that promise sooner than I ever imagined.

"I'm in awe of you right now. That's why I'm equal parts pissed and drawn to you," Langston tells a truth, surprising the hell out of us both.

"Why? We played the same game. We both did things that we had to in order to make it to the next round," I say.

He turns my head back to face him. His eyes carry a heaviness as he puts the sponge up to my bottom lip to wash the remnants of blood away.

"No, what I did doesn't compare to you."

I clear my throat, unsure of what to say to that. I never thought we'd be in a tub like this together, sharing an intimate moment. Even though I can feel the hardness of his cock against my ass, he hasn't tried to touch me inappropriately. He hasn't tried to kiss me, turn me on, or fuck me.

"I need to wash between your legs. I need you to be clean of any place that man touched before we get to the 'then' part."

I suck in air, knowing I'm going to need all of it. While he's touching me so intimately with the sponge, I won't be able to breathe.

I realize he's asking me for permission. This isn't something he's willing to take.

I nod.

His hand reaches around my waist with the sponge in his hand, and then he moves it in slow circles between my legs. The soft bristles cause enough friction that little zips of energy flutter in my stomach. Or maybe it's because of the man sitting behind me, caressing me so carefully.

"He also sucked my nipples," I say.

He growls low and even as his hand moves up to my breasts, and he rubs the sponge over each. This time harder than he did between my legs.

I bite back a moan. It shouldn't feel this good. Nothing this man does should feel good.

Without thinking, I grab his wrist when he tries to pull away.

I immediately release him, though, but not before he mutters 'fuck' under his breath.

I affect him just like he does me.

Even if we were good, kind, do-gooders, we shouldn't be together. He's dynamite, and I'm fire. You can't combine the two without destroying everything and everyone—ourselves included.

Langston puts the sponge down on the edge of the tub.

First, he wants to wash me.

Then, he wants to...

"Then?" I ask, not sure I can handle his answer.

"Then, we both come."

14
LANGSTON

I KNEW SITTING in the tub would lower her guard, make her more willing to do the next part we both crave. But I didn't think it would also lower my own defenses.

I can't think around Liesel.

All I can do is suck in air by the gallon and hope it's enough to survive.

Neither of us has spoken since I said the word come.

We can't.

Our brains are consumed with scolding fire and hurricane winds fighting through our bodies. That's how badly we both need to come.

I haven't decided whether we will be making the other come or doing it ourselves.

I don't fucking care.

I just need to explode in this tub, and I need to see her come undone more than I need my heart to keep thumping. I wouldn't live long if my heart stopped, but seeing her face as she falls apart in a glorious orgasm would be worth it.

She scoots away from me in the tub, and I let her. She wants a few moments to process what I just said. As much as

I hate the cold feeling as she leaves my skin, I let her go to the other side of the tub.

"What did you say?" she asks.

"You heard me."

"Tomorrow night is going to be non-stop sex. I don't think we need to worry about a release tonight."

I raise my eyebrows. "Do you really think any man or woman left has the ability to make you come? I'm not even sure all that moaning with Waylon was real. You're a difficult woman to please, Liesel Dunn."

She glares at me. "And you think you are capable?"

"I am, but that's not what I'm saying. I can make you come, or you can do it yourself. But I want to know what you really sound like when you come. So tomorrow, when you are moaning and faking it, I'll know the truth."

She licks her bottom lip, and I know she won't say no. Even though she made herself come earlier, she reacted so sensitively to my touch. She's still too wound up to sleep, same as me.

"We shouldn't," Liesel whispers.

She doesn't say why we shouldn't—we both know. *It would ruin everything.*

Things we know.

Things we don't know.

Things we assume but haven't spoken aloud.

But there is also a twinkle in her eye, a mischief, a wanting desire that the girl I used to know would give me. The woman in front of me now shows it in a much dirtier way.

She wants to come as much or more than I do.

I watch as her hand dips into the water between her legs. Her hooded eyes look up at me, and her breath slows and shallows. She doesn't wait for me to start, for me to tell her touch herself. She took control of the situation.

Clearly, the only way she can come is if she's in control.

I'll let her have that control tonight, because I want to watch her come in pieces. I need to hear the ecstasy she feels as she moans and calls out—in person, not over a monitor. Not through a closet.

Tomorrow though, I'll use this little tidbit against her. All I have to do to beat her is take the control.

Liesel is already broken, so taking control won't break her; it will just burst the stitches holding together the illusion that she's whole.

"Are you going to touch yourself, too, or am I doing this by myself?"

I chuckle.

"Need to see my cock in order to come?"

She bats her eyelashes. "I don't need a man for anything. But looking at your filthy cock won't hurt, even if it's not as impressive as the guys I'm used to."

My hands grip the side of the tub as I raise myself above the water and sit on the edge, so she can see just how unimpressive my cock is, according to her. I smirk, and my eyes threaten of what I want to do to her, of what I should do to her.

She gasps when our eyes meet.

"Killer, don't...not tonight..."

Tomorrow.

We both know we will make it to the finals. Tomorrow we will finally fuck each other, hurt each other. Fight each other to win the battle she entered us in.

I nod solemnly, agreeing to her terms.

She exhales harshly, her shoulders slumping.

I grab my cock, holding it loosely in my hand.

Her eyes are locked on my hand as she rubs between her submerged legs.

"Show me," I say. I won't be able to keep my hands off her if I can't see her come.

She licks her bottom lip, considering my command. Then she hops up on the tub edge opposite me. She spreads her legs wide as he lifts one leg up onto the side of the tub, giving me an even better view.

Her lips are swollen pink. Her pussy is bare. Her perfectly manicured fingers slip between her legs and into her tight slit. When she removes her two fingers, I can see the sticky evidence of how turned on she is on her fingers. Her moisture is dripping from her pussy down to her ass.

"Fuck," I breathe.

She smiles at my reaction. "Like what you see?"

I glance down at my cock that has somehow grown harder. *Painfully harder.*

I pump my cock, showing her how much I appreciate the show.

Her soft moan hits me in the chest, making me ache to touch her. *God, why did I agree to not touch her again?*

"Do you like it soft and slow or hard and fast?" I ask.

"I like it in control, without pain, but then you already know that. You?"

"I like being in control, too."

She rubs over her clit, her head falling back until she's no longer looking at me. "Which is one of the many reasons why we shouldn't ever fuck. We can't both be in control. All we'd end up doing is hurting each other."

I snort. "We hurt each other plenty without fucking."

Her eyes roll back to me. She's breathless, her cheeks are a light pink, and the way she's biting on her bottom lip and no longer speaking shows how close she is to coming. She stops moving her fingers quickly over her clit. She slows to the point there is no way she'll come.

"You first," she pants.

"I thought it was ladies first?"

"I'm not showing you how incredible I look when I come until you show me how much of the devil escapes your soul when you do."

I pump faster, letting my gaze roam her body and pretend her hand is the one stroking my cock. I have no problem being the one who comes first.

Faster, faster I stroke until warm white liquid shoots from my cock, splashing in the water between us.

As soon as I come, she loses it. One more circular motion of her fingers over her clit, and she's crying out in soft explosive moans.

I try to soak in everything. Her face opening wide as if she's letting all of the pain out. Her breasts heaving up and down. Her opening is contracting around her fingers, soaking them in her come.

It's too much and too little. I want more. I want to feel her as she comes. Taste her. Smell her.

For now, seeing will have to be enough.

Slowly, she comes back to earth. While she came, she was her most vulnerable. I could have asked her any question, done anything to her, and she would have let me.

I tuck that secret away for another time. I'm not sure I'm strong enough to take advantage of her like that, but I will if I have to.

I lean forward.

"You got it wrong. The devil doesn't escape me when I come. More of the devil enters my soul until I'm more evil than anything else."

I grab her hand where her fingers are still buried in her pussy. Slowly, I remove them, watching her body reluctantly release her fingers and spill out cum. Then I lift her hand to my mouth, and I suck her fingers clean.

I got to see her come. I got a taste and smell of her cum. Now all I need is to feel.

That will be the last thing I take from her.

She swallows hard, like her throat is on fire.

"I think I liked the then part the most," she says.

I agree.

"Finally, I want to hear all your lies. This changes nothing. I still want to kill you."

15
LIESEL

Every sexual encounter with Langston is hotter than the previous.

He didn't even touch me until after I had already come, but rubbing myself while he was watching me, while he was stroking himself, while he was so close—*fuck me.*

Those words almost slipped from my lips so many times.

My body was screaming for Langston to fuck me.

Fuck me.

Fuck me.

Fuck me.

For the first time, I wasn't sure if it mattered if I was in control or not. It didn't matter if Langston tied me up and stripped me of all my power. It didn't matter if he pushed his cock between my lips, in my ass, or in my cunt. All I wanted was his cock inside me. His lips kissing me. His hands touching me.

Every time I'm around Langston, I want more.

And every time I realize just how bad things would get if we were to cross that line into more.

Langston steps out of the tub and grabs a fluffy towel

from the nearby shelf. He doesn't grab one for me or help me in any way.

I stand and grab another towel. I dry quickly before grabbing the single white robe hanging on the back of the bathroom door and wrapping it around me. I walk into the bedroom after Langston.

I don't see him.

Did he leave?

My heart flutters at that. I both want him to have left and want him to still be here.

I turn to the right and see Langston out of the corner of my eye, sitting in one of the two chairs on my balcony.

I exhale.

He didn't leave.

I hesitate before I walk over to him, trying to prepare myself for the conversation.

Langston wants me to lie. He wants me to give him another reason to hate me, to eventually kill me.

I'll lie alright. But it will be closer to the truth than he'll ever know.

I slide the door open and step outside. Wordlessly, I take the seat next to him.

When I glance over, I see he's shirtless with only the towel wrapped around his waist.

Jesus.

How does he think I'm going to be able to focus on anything?

"So tell me, how does a girl who grew up with a whore for a mother decide the only way to make money is to whore herself out now?"

I slap him again.

He's made comments like this before, but I'm not tolerating it.

"I am not a whore."

He smirks. "Why did you enter this game, then? You've been here before. You've played before, won before. Why?"

I drag my eyes from him to the ocean. "Is this the part where I'm supposed to lie so I can fuel your sick rage to eventually kill me?"

He shrugs. "Ultimately, it's up to you whether you tell the truth or lie."

"Lie it is then," I say.

His jaw ticks, but otherwise, he remains stone-faced.

"I've been living in hell since I was eighteen years old." The year that Langston left me. That was the year my world changed. Since then, nothing has been the same.

"Liar. You thrived after I left you," Langston says.

He has no idea what happened after I left, the deal I made. And he never will.

"Be quiet and let me tell the story. Otherwise, I'll stop talking right now."

He rolls his eyes but doesn't speak again.

"As I was saying, I'd already been living in hell for years. My entire life has been dealing with the flames of the devil. Some years were harder than others, but then I met Duncan."

"Who is he?"

"So impatient."

"Duncan is the man who brought me here."

Langston frowns. "Against your will?"

I laugh. "I don't do anything against my will, not anymore. I wanted money—knowing it was the only way I could ensure that I never had to do anything against my will again."

"So you whored yourself out?" he asks.

"Do you want me to slap you again?"

He chuckles and puts his hands up in surrender.

"I didn't know I was whoring myself out. He brought me

here. Told me there was a game he thought I'd enjoy, and I could feel in control. He said it would bring me enough wealth that I would never have to worry again."

"Did he tell you what you were signing up for?"

"Yes and no. He asked how far I'd be willing to go to earn unlimited freedom. I said as far as it takes."

I pause.

Langston's body is hard as stone, and his eyes have rage spelled out in his pupils.

"I understood what he wasn't saying. I could read between the lines. It was my choice to come here, to play the game."

"And he demanded a cut?"

My eyes gloss over. *Yes. No.* I can't think about that—about all of the fucking pain. I'd break more than I already have. I may not be able to get through tomorrow or tonight as it is.

"No, I took everything I won." A sly smile spreads. "And I won everything."

Langston's lips turn up into not quite a smile, but I know he's impressed by me.

"Where's the lie?" he asks after a beat.

"That's for you to figure out."

Everything. Almost everything is a lie, yet not enough is.

We sit in uncomfortable silence for a while, both staring out at the ocean.

"So how much time are you taking off? Another month? Six months? You plan on killing me tomorrow?" I finally ask, not hiding the disdain in my voice.

He sighs, and there is an emotion on his face that I haven't seen since we were kids—fear.

"What happens tomorrow, huntress? How do you survive if I don't save you like I did tonight?" Langston asks, referring to him kicking Zeke out of the games.

I shake my head. "You don't understand how different tomorrow's games will be."

"Tell me."

"It's not something I can tell. It's only something you can experience."

He frowns. "Huntress…"

"You can't save me. No one can. And I don't need you to. Only I can save myself."

Langston gets up and walks to the sliding door.

"What happens when we both make it to the final round?" he asks as he pauses at the door.

I lose.

"I hope you make it to the final round with me. I'd love to see you go through hell," I reply.

16
LANGSTON

WHY DID I go see her last night?

It was a mistake. Now I can't do anything but think of her. Of her body, the sounds she made when she came. She has crept into every part of my body all day.

It's more than that, though. I've played her little story in my head over and over, and I can't figure out the lie. I also can't figure out who Duncan is.

It's probably because he doesn't exist. That's the lie—his name. That way, I can't look up to see who she's working with.

I throw my phone in frustration after once again coming up empty on my search for information on the owners of this yacht and fucked up game.

There is a knock at my door.

I huff as I stand and walk over to it.

"Yes?" I answer while throwing the door open.

Beckett is standing in my doorway with a stack of two to-go coffee cups and a raised eyebrow. I'm always impressed with how he's adapted to a life with only one arm.

"You look like hell," he says as he pushes the top cup into my hands and walks inside my room.

"Thanks," I say. The hot liquid runs down my throat while I hope it turns everything around for me. It's only a couple hours until midnight, but I'm going to need the coffee to stay awake all night, especially since I haven't slept.

"Couldn't sleep?" he asks.

"Yea, Liesel got into my head." I run my hand through my hair, messing it up even more.

"Women." Beckett shakes his head like he doesn't understand why I'd ever let a woman bother me. "You and Liesel aren't together though, right? So why do you let her affect you so much?"

"Our relationship is complicated. I want to kill her most of the time."

"But you also want to fuck her?" Beckett says with a grin.

"Something like that," I grump.

"But you don't love her?"

"No." *I could never love her.*

"Hmmm, then fuck her and get over her."

If only it were that easy.

"What about you and Nora? Isn't she going to be pissed that you let some woman suck your dick?"

"I actually fucked the second woman."

I frown. *Nora will kill him.* "You need to withdraw. I don't want to ruin any more relationships than I have to. I'll be alright. I don't need anyone to stay in the game just for me."

"Nora and I broke up. I'm a free man. And I plan on staying and helping for as long as I can. So far, I've quite enjoyed myself."

I chuckle. "Well, I'm sorry about you and Nora."

He shrugs. "I'm not. It was fun while it lasted, but we were never meant to be together."

"You don't have to be loyal to me just because I work with your brother."

"I'm not. You're as much a part of this family as I am. And we protect our family."

I nod, thankful that I have someone here. I have no idea what tonight holds. Beckett and I have never been as close as any other pair in the group, but I'm thankful nonetheless.

"Don't push yourself too far tonight to defeat Liesel. If she wins, we can steal the money again like before," Beckett says nonchalantly.

We can't.

And I'm beginning to think I need to win for more reasons than just keeping the money from Liesel. Something feels off about everything Liesel said last night. It feels like she's begging for help, for a way to escape. I want her dead, but at my hands. No one else gets to bury Liesel except for me.

A few minutes later, Beckett leaves. I take my time getting dressed once again in my suit that has somehow been dry cleaned and delivered to my room. Then I don the mask, tying it around the upper half of my face.

The mask is supposed to make me feel invincible, discreet and hidden. I hate hiding, though. I'd rather fight head-on. I didn't give a fake name when we boarded, because I'd rather everyone know exactly who I am. Hopefully, I can take my mask off in the final round.

I glance at the clock in my room—a quarter till midnight.

Showtime.

I walk into the hallway and up the stairs, the caffeine buzzing through my body, making me feel alive and ready.

I'm ready for whatever I face tonight.

When I reach the top deck, the air feels different than last night. Last night everyone was chatting; there was a nervous, excited energy about the crowd. Tonight, it's all anxious nerves. There is no small talk between the eight remaining participants. Only about half the people up here even have a drink in their hand. Everyone has a solemn, ready to go to war look in their eyes.

Everyone left came to win.

"It feels eery up here. I feel like everyone here knows what's about to happen except for us," Beckett whispers.

I nod. I feel the same.

There are five men, including Beckett and myself.

Two women.

And…

Liesel.

I tried to ignore the pull I felt when I stepped foot up here, but it's here, plain as day.

She's wearing a different dress than last night. This one is all black, and she has a black mask. The only thing that isn't black on her body is her dark red lipstick.

How did she get a new dress?

Everyone else here is wearing a dry cleaned version of what they wore the night before.

What game is this, Liesel? Why did I let my anger out last night? I should have demanded a truth instead of a lie. Then I might have a damn clue what this stupid game is.

I look at Liesel, trying to gain any insight from her expression. I find nothing. She's solid stone. Expressionless and unbending.

I stare her down. *I'm going to destroy you, and then I'm going to take you back to my island, and we are going to finish what we started.*

"Congratulations, everyone, on making it to the second night," Mr. Reyes says, holding a glass of champagne in his hand.

An employee carries a tray of champagne glasses around the deck, offering a glass to everyone.

I turn it down. I don't want to drink sweet champagne right now.

"Tonight will be much different than last night. Last night was about dipping your toes into this world. Tonight, you'll dive headfirst into the deep end." He smirks like he knows a secret that will ruin all of us.

I grind my teeth and my hands fist. *Out with it!*

"Last night you had complete control over the situation. Tonight, you'll lose all control. The only power you'll be able to wield is the ability to say your safe word and leave the game."

I glance at Liesel again. She can't lose control. I can't lose control.

How are we going to survive?

Liesel looks into my soul. *We won't.*

Fuck.

"Tonight, I'll draw names to decide your partner each round, but that partner won't be the one pushing you. The owner of the game will be selecting a challenge for each of you. You won't be fighting against each other. You'll be fighting against yourself. Your worst demons. The darkest part of your soul."

I've fucked plenty of women in my life. Phoenix and I may be legally married, but we aren't tied to only fuck each other. We aren't lovers in that sense. *Have we fucked? Yes.* But it's never crossed to love or loyalty to each other.

I'm a free man. I can fuck whoever and whenever and however I want. I can't imagine a sexual act that I wouldn't be willing to do, not if it meant destroying Liesel a little more.

Bring it on.

"The rules are also different tonight. There are two ways you get knocked out of the game—either by using your safe word or by not completing the challenge. Once you are knocked out, you will get to watch the rest of the games from a safe room. Any questions?"

The room is silent. I have so many, but I'm not going to ask any of them. I'm not going to appear weak in any way.

I haven't been weak since I was a boy.

Never again.

Mr. Reyes starts pairing off people, until there are only four of us left: Liesel, me, Beckett, and another man.

I exhale.

I don't even know who I want to be paired with anymore.

"Ms. White and Mr. Beckett."

Liesel and Beckett are paired together.

Beckett gives me a cocky wink as he walks toward her. I don't think I can handle the two of them together.

A low growl escapes. It's a territorial growl, but Beckett takes the hint.

He nods once.

That leaves me and the remaining man to be paired.

I have nothing against men fucking each other; I'm just not gay. But I have a feeling this isn't about who you're partnered with. This is going to be different. I just don't understand how.

"The first and the last couples drawn will go first. Each of you will be led to the two rooms where you will be completing your challenges, while the rest of you will be led to the viewing area. Once the challenges are finished, you'll swap places."

That means Liesel will be able to watch me, and I'll be able to watch her.

"Gentleman, if you'll follow me," a woman in a simple black dress says. She's not wearing a mask, the clue that she's an employee and not a player.

We follow her down from the top to the bottom deck. It

feels like we are walking down into a dungeon, possibly to our deaths as we descend deeper into the ship.

She opens a door and holds it open for us as we step inside. The room is about twice the size of the bedrooms on the ship. It has a king-sized bed in the center, but otherwise, there are no whips, chains, bludgeons—nothing that makes it seem anything other than an ordinary bedroom. The only light comes from two light shades on either side of the bed. There are no windows or other light sources I can see.

The woman steps in after us and closes the door behind her.

"Mr. Pearce, this challenge is for you. You'll have five minutes to mentally prepare, and then the challenge will start. You are required to do and accept everything on the card to complete your challenge. Understand?"

"Yes."

She smiles tightly. "Here you go. You have five minutes." She hands me a standard-sized index card.

I read through it quickly as my skin turns pale.

How?

I'm going to kill Liesel. She had to have told someone who I am and about my past. That's the only way they could have picked out this specific challenge for me. Although, I stupidly gave my real name and made it simple for them to find me.

The card is basically all of my fears thrown into one twisted game.

They know I was beaten as a kid.

And that's exactly what I have to do—beat another and then get beaten while climaxing.

Who thinks up these sick challenges?

I glance up in the corner of the room, looking for a camera, but I find none. My eyes cut around the room; the wall seems completely flat. I don't see any indication of a camera, but there must be one somewhere.

The man who is partnered with me sits on the edge of the bed. He wasn't given any instructions. He doesn't know what my challenge is.

I have less than five minutes to decide if I'm going to do this task or not.

Liesel, what did you do? What horror will your task be?

She'll do it, whatever it is. She's done it before. This round can't be any worse than what she's already done.

Why?

What the hell am I missing? There has to be easier ways to get money.

I close my eyes in thought. I'm already going to hell; *what difference does it make if I do this?* This man is a man, not a boy. He can say his safe word and stop. This is for millions of dollars. This is to stop Liesel. This is for so much more...

When I open my eyes, it's like the room has transformed.

Smoke has started to billow in, making it hard for me to see anything except a small table that has been placed in front of me with a man's belt lying on it.

They couldn't even give me a whip; they had to give me a belt—my father's tool of choice.

You can do this. This is just like any other time you've beaten a criminal for information. This will be no different. The man who is playing isn't a good person. If he was, he wouldn't be here.

I walk over to the table with the belt. There is a single white card attached to it. I yank it off.

20 lashings with the belt.

20 with your fist.

Repeat until he breaks, until he uses his safe word.

. . .

Fuck.

This is about me or him.

Either I win or he does.

Don't show weakness. You're giving a grown man a lashing—something you experienced nightly as a child.

Liesel was right; I'll be living through hell. As much as I don't want to do the first part, the second part is what is going to fuck with my mind. The second part is going to try and twist my worst nightmare with sex. I may never be able to fuck normally again.

The smoke parts, and I see my partner. Except I'm not sure he's my partner. He looks younger. He's no longer in a suit; he's in shorts and a T-shirt. He seems smaller, weaker. He wears a new mask, one that isn't as dark. This one is white, pure.

He's a grown man. He's not a child. But damn did they do a good job of tricking my mind.

"Begin," a man's deep voice comes through a speaker in the room.

At the sound of his unfamiliar voice, I decide I'm going to see this through. I realize the voice must somehow be that of someone I know. If he's the one in charge of these games, then the only way to meet and destroy him is to win.

I'm now more determined than ever to win.

I smirk.

I probably look like a sadistic asshole. But when I do this challenge, all I'll be thinking about is the voice. How he screwed up by letting me play these games. I will win and will end his life.

I pick up the belt.

It feels strange in my hands. My head wants to start making the connection to my father, but I don't let it.

All I think about is him—the guy behind the voice.

He used his voice to threaten me. To make me feel small, but it fueled everything inside me.

I crack the belt across the man's back—striking with everything I can. The best way to win is to start strong. To make him think this is only my first gear, that I can go higher, hit harder. Put the fear into him. Fear that he won't be able to survive. That he won't know when this stops. He didn't get a card. He has no clue how long he has to endure, which I realize must be his challenge.

He doesn't know that if he survives, the roles will be reversed except so much worse for me. I have to find a way to make my body come while enduring the pain.

Stop thinking.

I hit again—two.

Three.

Four.

Five.

I act cool and collected with each strike. I don't grunt or show any sound of strain as I use the belt to hit him. I'm silent. I'm composed. In my head, I'm thinking of all the ways I'll kill the voice.

Twenty.

Now for twenty hits with my fist.

This is actually easier for me. I'm used to fighting with my fists. It actually makes it less personal. And maybe the guy will fight back—that would make me fight on instinct instead of hitting him because a damn card told me to.

I carefully place the belt back on the table, hoping I won't have to pick it up again. And then I walk toward the man, every footstep loud and heavy, telling him of his impending doom.

Say the damn safe word, my steps say.

I won't.

You will.

Say it, and I won't beat you to within a second of your life.

Say it, and you get to live.

I should hit him while he's down. That's how you beat a man, but I'm not my father.

I yank him up by the back of his shirt until he's standing in front of me. I see the blood on his back, soaking his white T-shirt. That's why they made him dress in white, so I could see the pain I inflicted on him.

When I look at him, face to face, I realize that he too got instructions somehow. He wouldn't be staying here if he didn't. He doesn't want to lose his challenge, but tears are streaming down his cheeks.

"Welcome to my world," I mutter sadly. This man would have broken a long time ago if he had to face my life. I've had a lifetime of this. He's endured five minutes.

"Fight me, it will make it easier to take," I say. That was a lesson I learned too late. I used to grow quiet, meek when my father raged on me. I used to just submit and obey. It took me too long to realize that it didn't lessen my suffering. It didn't make him hit me any lighter, and by submitting, I just felt helpless.

My eyes glisten with the truth.

I know he sees it.

He lifts his fists in front of his face, and I know he wants to fight me. But then he immediately drops them.

If I wanted confirmation that this is part of his challenge, I just got it. He's not allowed to fight. I don't know what his demons are, but this is part of it.

Jesus Christ.

This is sick.

But it's him or me. And a twisted part of me knows this is for the greater good. If he were to win the whole game, he wouldn't be able to take the bastard down. I would. I don't have a choice but to win.

I ball my hand into a fist, giving him my only warning.

Say your damn safe word, and let's end this.

He closes his eyes.

I sigh; that will just make his fear worse. His body won't be prepared for the hit.

I swing with everything I have, aiming for the hinge of his jaw. I hear it crack. He falls back, blood spills from his mouth, and he lands hard on his ass.

I know how painful it is. I've broken my jaw before. It was a pain to reset and heal. The best way to do that is to stitch it shut for weeks at a time, not something I was willing to do. I assume that's why my smile is more crooked than it ever was before.

I wait for him to move, for him to get back up so I can knock him down again. That will mess with his head and soul. That will defeat him quicker than any pain will.

But he doesn't get back up.

I walk over to him and lean down, putting a finger to his neck.

There's a pulse, but it's weak. His breathing is shallow.

His eyes don't open.

He's unconscious.

I stand up and look around the room.

The card said to continue until he breaks. Until he uses his safe word.

The sucker is definitely broken, but he won't be saying his safe word any time soon.

I'm the devil, but I'm not so monstrous that I'll hit a man when he's unconscious, especially a man whose sins I don't know.

I take a deep breath. I'm barely breaking a sweat even though I'm still wearing a suit and living my nightmare.

"Mr. Pearce, you have a five-minute break. You can clear the room while we tend to Mr. Newman. Then we will continue," the vile motherfucker's voice says again.

The smoke fills my lungs and burns my eyes as I walk to the door at the back. Even though I can't see, I walk straight to the door.

It unlocks as I push on it, and then I'm in the hallway, able to truly breathe for the first time.

I only have five minutes. I don't know where to go or what to do with that time. But I decide to climb, to get fresh air, to look out at the sea—the place that saves everyone in my group when we need it the most—Kai, Enzo, Zeke, Siren. It's saved all of them at different times. Now it's time it saves me.

I cling to the railing as I stare out at the ocean. For a split second, I consider jumping. But I don't. I just hold on, preparing myself for what comes next.

"I'm sorry," her soft sweet voice comes next to me.

I don't know if she's real or a hallucination.

"I shouldn't have come back here. I forgot how bad it can get. This is only the beginning. It can get so much worse," she says.

"How do we survive?" I ask the same question I asked before.

"We don't. Only one of us does, and that person will be haunted forever. Let that person be me. You don't deserve this pain."

Liesel's words mean I have to win even more.

She'll never tell me the truth of what this place is or what happens when you win, but I have to know. I need to know.

I enter the room once more, still not completely sure if

Liesel showing up was real or a hallucination I formed to help me deal with this traumatic cruise.

Once I'm back in the room, though, any thoughts of Liesel disappear.

In here, the only way to win is to stay focused.

The room is still filled with smoke when I re-enter. I blink, trying to keep the smoke from my eyes. My nose immediately fills with the haze, making it hard to breathe.

Messing with our senses is meant to strike fear, but my fear is gone.

I walk further into the center of the room, where I once again find the table with the index card. I pick it up. It has more detailed instructions for the second half of the challenge.

Take a beating. Endure any pain given to you. This round ends when you come or say your safe word.

I glance around the room, but I don't find anyone. Mr. Newman is gone. I'm guessing he's still unconscious, and hopefully, a doctor is attending to him.

Who will be giving me my lashing?

I don't see the belt I used before, but I'm guessing it's somewhere. I also don't see the bed.

"I hope you are ready for this round, Mr. Pearce. This will be your biggest challenge yet. The games begin, now," the voice comes over the speakers again.

I want to flip him off, run through the ship to find him and kill him. But I'd never get to him before he killed me. He's too secure where he is. The only way I find the voice at the other end of the speaker is to win.

Let's get this over with.

People run into the room in a flurry. Between the smoke, rush of people, and now lights flashing in my face, it takes me a moment to count how many people are in the room.

Four.

Two men.

Two women.

Jesus, this isn't just a man whipping me like I did to Newman.

Before I can fully process what's happening, the two women are removing my coat jacket, then one is unbuttoning my shirt, while the other works on my pants.

It's not the women I'm worried about. I can overpower them easily. It's the men.

I was told to endure and come, but no one said anything about not fighting back.

Within seconds, I'm stripped of my clothes, and then the women are gone. I think they are still in the room, but they are no longer touching me now that my clothes are off.

I focus in on the guys. They are boxing me in on each side. I could take the two of them.

No.

Let them come.

Let them hurt me.

That's what has to happen for this to be over, in order for me to win.

I let them attack.

They run at me like they are afraid I'll put up a fight. It takes everything in me to not knock them both out, to not resist.

I close my eyes, but that only intensifies their movements in my head. I try meditating as they come for me. I think they are going to tie me up, but they stop just short. That's when I feel the cracking of belts on my back.

The familiar feeling of my dad's belt on me creeps back

into my muscle memory. I feel everything just like I did as a child.

They aren't hitting me that hard. The pain is doable. The problem is the haunting memories playing in my head like a movie.

My dad's voice.

His hand grabbing me.

His belt hitting me.

I open my eyes, hoping the memories will fade.

I jolt forward as a belt hits my back. This one was harder than the previous ones, but still not enough to make my eyes water, my pulse to race, or my body to send signals to my brain to fight back.

The two women start approaching me, and I remember the other part of my challenge.

I have to come.

I glance down, but I don't have to to know that I am zero percent turned on. Coming right now seems almost impossible. Even if both women start sucking and licking and giving me the best strip show of my life, it won't be enough.

I should give up now, rather than be tortured like this.

But his voice.

Knowing who he is...

I have to win. I don't have a choice.

I welcome the women in as I collapse to my knees with my cock in my hand. I try to stroke my cock like I did only hours ago in Liesel's bathroom.

My body doesn't respond. My cock is limp in my hands.

"We can help you out there," one of the women says as they reach me. They are wearing lingerie. One has a black, lace bra and thong complete with a garter. The other woman is wearing a white flowy number.

I suppose they are supposed to fulfill whatever my

fantasies are. Whether I like a bad girl or an angel—I have both.

Their hands start roaming over my chest as the men continue to hit my back over and over with the belts. Not exactly inflicting pain, but delivering a constant thread of nightmares.

I try to focus on the women.

Their touch.

Their smell.

Their bodies.

I can't feel any of it.

I'm back in the house I grew up in. My father is beating me because he ran out of beer.

The back door opens just as my father is about to hit me again.

Liesel is standing there, except she's no longer a child; she's the woman I know.

"What are you doing here?" I ask.

"Saving you." She smiles.

And then, she's running to me.

She scoops me up from the floor and carries me across the street to her couch.

Finally, I can breathe. My father can't hurt me here. Liesel's protecting me.

I half hiccup, half sob.

"Shh, it's okay. There is nothing to fear, not anymore. I'm here."

I nod.

I'm safe because of her.

Liesel climbs on top of me.

"What are you doing?"

"Loving you. We both need love. This is the only way."

The only way to what?

But then she's kissing me. Her long blonde hair is spilling

onto my cheeks and brushing against my neck as she kisses me. It's everything I wanted it to be and more.

So much more. It pushes out all the pain until all I feel is her.

And then I feel her hand grip my cock.

My eyes roll back. I've never been touched like this before.

It's heaven. It's everything.

It's…

17

LIESEL

I STIFLE my gasp by biting my lip and swallowing it down until it burns my throat.

I'm sitting in a room with six other participants watching Langston fall to the floor.

He passed out.

I look over at Beckett out of the corner of my eye, trying to gauge his reaction. But he's just as good at hiding his emotions as I am.

Beckett doesn't so much as speak.

I glance back at the large screen in front of us. The men whip him one more time after he collapses, and I want to barrel through the wall and rip their throats out.

Finally, they stop after they realize he's passed out.

The women step back.

I don't know what happened.

Watching him broke me more than whatever I will face next ever could.

I would've called out my safe word if it had a chance at stopping his madness. I don't know how they know our greatest fears and weaknesses, but they always find them here and exploit them. They did the last time I was here too.

Get up.

Get the fuck up, killer!

I watch, but Langston doesn't get up. *Does that mean he's disqualified?*

"Mr. Pearce will be advanced to the next round," the voice says. A voice that always sends chills down my spine.

How will Langston advance?

I stare at Langston more closely, and that's when I see the drop of cum on the floor.

Technically, he came.

A part of me wishes he had lost now. The rest of me wants him to win so he can kick everyone involved in this organization's ass.

But I need the money. I need to win.

Langston is the only person standing between me and victory. Right now, all I can do is beg him to wake up. To show me he's still alive—that this didn't ruin him forever like it did me.

Finally, a couple of men walk over to him. Langston's back is covered in red welts, and there are a few drops of blood, but it doesn't look like they did any permanent damage to his back.

They hook their arms under his and lift him up.

I lean forward in my chair as I stare at a man I thought could never be broken.

Please, don't be broken. Please, please, please.

Langston is slumped in their arms, only being held up because of the men's strength, not his own. He's completely naked. He looks like he just walked through hell, and his limp body is all that is left of him.

I want them to cover him up, to show him some dignity. I know they won't, though.

Slowly, Langston starts to awaken. His head rolls side to side. At first, he doesn't have the strength to even lift his head. But he won't let anyone see him as weak.

It takes everything in him, but he lifts his head up, and then it's like he's looking right at me into a nearby camera. He's telling me he's fine. That he isn't broken. That he survived. And I was the one who helped him survive.

Me.

I'm whom he thought about to get through it.

Not Phoenix.

Not Siren.

Not some other whore.

Not his kids.

Me.

I don't know what to do with that information. It's a lot to take.

Finally, Langston is led out of the room, and we can no longer see him. I know from experience he will be given a room where he can shower, take a hot bath, eat some food, and drink some coffee. There is also a screen to watch the rest of the round if he so chooses.

He's safe now.

Just for now, not for later. Later is the opposite of safe.

What did I do? Why did I bring him here?

I didn't, he followed. This isn't my fault.

At least, that's what I keep telling myself.

"Ms. White and Mr. Beckett, your turn," Mr. Reyes says, entering the room.

We both nod, but don't show any emotion. Soon one or both of us is going to be as beat up and broken as Langston. I hope Beckett realizes what he's gotten himself into now.

He can still stop this before it goes too far. I don't know what his trauma is, but everyone has trauma. Everyone has a past they are running from—Beckett is no different.

I only know pieces of his story. He's the half brother of Enzo Black. Their family is darker than any I know. Beckett's full name is Eli Beckett, but he's always gone by his last name. I know that he's close to Enzo's kids. I don't know how he lost his arm, just that he helped to save Enzo and Kai. Once he did that, he became more a part of the group than I ever could be.

I don't want to belong to their criminal gang. I've tried most of my life to get out, to stop belonging. Now I finally succeeded. They all entered the game just to show me how much they hate me and are on Langston's side.

Beckett remained till the end. I thought he had a woman he cared about. *Nora, was it?* Apparently, they aren't that close.

"If you're ready, you can follow me, Ms. White and Mr. Beckett," Mr. Reyes says.

We both stand at the same time. Beckett holds his hand out to indicate I should go first.

I follow Mr. Reyes while Beckett walks behind me.

I have a few ideas of what awaits me in the room now that it's my turn. I've been here before. They know my weaknesses, my strengths, and my fears.

We enter the room, and Mr. Reyes locks the door behind us.

Beckett and I exchange glances, knowing the lines we will cross if we both try to win this game. I don't give a damn who tortures me, who fucks me. As long as it's not Langston, it doesn't matter.

There are two white, labeled cards on the small table in the center of the room. We walk over and pick up our respective card, neither of us letting the other see what's on our own card.

I read mine:

. . .

White,

You already knew what this round would be—a rematch of your last round here. You survived once, but can you survive again?

X

I grip the paper tightly in my hand, crumpling it into a little ball.

I never got over what happened here the last time. To relive it would be my greatest hell. It's one thing to go through it once and survive. It's another to know exactly what's coming, to have visions of the last time haunting my head while it's happening again, and to not mutter my safe word.

I still haven't looked at my safe word. I won't until the final round. I've already made the choice. I'll finish this round. I'll either die or win. There is no pulling myself out.

I glance over at Beckett, who has a stern expression under his black mask.

He doesn't like what's on his card either.

I don't care if he stays or leaves. My card will be carried out whether he continues the game or not, just like what happened to Langston.

I try to think of Langston, try to let my thoughts drift to him, soaking his wounds in a warm tub right now.

It makes me smile.

Langston may be my enemy, and he may be the devil, but he's slipped through my defenses to wiggle a tiny piece of himself into my heart. I can't help but care a little about the bastard.

Plus, holding onto any positive thoughts of Langston for as long as I can will help me. Or it will twist him deeper into my soul and make me hate him more…

"You have five minutes to prepare," the familiar voice announces.

I don't need five minutes, but it gives me time to be in control.

I reach behind my head, and I remove my mask, lying it carefully on the table. I kick off my heels, too. Unfortunately, I'm going to need Beckett's help for the next part.

"Can you help me unzip my dress?" I ask him.

He stands frozen, looking at me like he thinks he just imagined me speaking. He's probably in shock from what is on his card.

I sigh, *poor man.*

I walk over to him and take his card.

"What are you doing?"

"Saving you for the next five minutes."

I crinkle his card into a ball and toss it on the floor. It makes a satisfying bounce as it slides away from us. Then I take Beckett's hand.

"Help me, and I'll help you."

He frowns.

I smile.

"The only thing I need help with is unzipping my dress."

"Did your card say…?"

I shake my head. "My card didn't say that I couldn't undress before it starts. If it isn't clearly on the card, then it's fair game. Now, are you going to help me?"

He nods.

I release his hand and turn around, lifting my black hair up. I hate the stupid wig, but it's necessary.

I feel his cold hand graze my back as he unzips my dress.

I turn back around and face him. "Thank you."

Then I shimmy out of the dress.

Beckett trains his eyes on my face as I stand naked in

front of him, which makes me grin even wider at his adorableness.

"If you can't handle looking at my naked body, you should just say your safe word and get out now," I say.

He shakes his head as he removes his jacket and then starts unbuttoning his shirt. It's impressive how he can tackle things I take for granted with one hand. Everything is harder for him, doing everything one-handed.

Finally, he's naked in front of me too.

I, unlike him, let my eyes explore his body. I see the painful-looking scar where his arm was cut. I see the wounds on his torso that mix with the ripples of his abs and V. His long toned legs. I even look at his cock. In a matter of minutes, it could be inside me; it's only fair that I get to look at it. It's a good cock—thick, long, and veiny. But I don't get a thrill in my stomach looking at it. There is only one cock that has ever done that.

I'm sick.

"Say your safe word before this starts, Beckett. I don't need you to protect me. Neither does Langston. If you do this, trust me, there is no going back to the life you had before. This will be your life. Everything will bring you back to this."

He frowns, and then he leans in, so there is no possible way the cameras could pick up his next words. "I'll say my safe word, but only after I ensure you're safe first."

"Why are you protecting me?" I breathe.

"Langston will hate me if I don't."

It's because Langston asked him to, not because Beckett considers me part of the family. That is reserved for Langston.

"I'm warning you, Beckett. You saw what the game did to Langston. It will do the same to you."

He gives me a smug smile and then holds out the stub

that is all that is left of his arm. "I survived this. I can survive anything."

I hope he's right.

"The challenge begins now," the haunting voice says. A voice I've tried to rid my brain of so many times, but it's permanently etched into my ears.

I look at Beckett, and he looks at me.

No one enters the room, so I know what is on Beckett's card, what his first task is.

I won't hate him for it, but I won't be able to go near him after he does this. He'll set off my worst nightmares like no one else can.

I should make this easy on Beckett, but my body literally can't. I know the rules, and I can do anything—fight, try to escape, anything. I just have to survive.

I don't know how long I have in here. As long as it takes to break me once again, that's how long.

"Please," I whisper as Beckett takes a step toward me.

He stops at my word, like he wasn't expecting me to make this hard for him. He thought I'd submit. I'd let him tie me up, take all my senses away.

He doesn't know me at all if he thinks I'll just take that. I can't.

I have to fight.

I made a promise to myself I'd never stop fighting. I'd always be in control. I chose this game. I chose to be here. This isn't rape. And yet, I'll fight while they tie me up. I'll fight while they do unthinkable things to my body. It's the only way I can make sense of everything in my mind.

"Beckett, please."

My eyes water—they won't spill tears, but they'll get close.

His hand balls into a fist, his legs remain planted, his eyes dart side to side, trying to make sense of what I'm not saying.

But then he takes a step.

One single step toward me.

I run.

I know the door is locked, that it's a waste to try and break the door down. I learned that the last time. The only way I survive this is to run and outsmart Beckett.

I start running, knowing the smoke will start soon, which might assist me in hiding from him.

The smoke creeps in, but all it does is make me break out in nervous hives—memories flood my head.

Out!

I stay focused on my goal—run until I can't run anymore. I hope to find a bed, some piece of furniture I can use either as a weapon or to hide under while I make my next move.

I find nothing.

It will be exactly the same as before.

You are strong.

You are powerful.

You are in control.

You can block out all evil with your mind.

I feel Beckett's hand grab onto my hair.

I was so close to getting caught. Luckily, I'm still wearing the black wig, so all Beckett grabs is the wig, and I keep running.

That was too close.

My time is running out.

Beckett is better than the last man who chased me. He's faster, smarter.

I should give up.

I can't give up.

I run.

Run.

RUN.

My hair falls from the bun—loose and free. Something I'll never be.

It will be my downfall—I know it before it happens.

I feel the tug on the back of my head, my feet stop in their tracks, and my body slings back as Beckett pulls me tight to his body, still holding on by my hair.

"I'm sorry," he whispers.

"Me too," I say back. I'm already broken. Technically, I've been broken since Enzo's dad raped me. But it didn't have to be this way for Beckett.

He starts dragging me by the hair. I grab onto his hand with mine and sink my nails into him.

He hisses but doesn't release me.

"You know you can save us both. Just say your safe word, and I'll say mine as well," Beckett moans in my ear as I feel little droplets of his blood dripping from his hand.

"I can't."

"Yes, you can."

"I don't know my safe word. I won't read it until the final round."

He gasps. "Fuck."

I feel him loosen his grasp, and I try to scramble away. My hair starts to slip through his fingers, almost to the end before he tightens his grip again.

Beckett's decision has been made. He'll do this for as long as he can, until he's pushed to a limit that Langston would kill him for crossing.

We both look at each other through the smoke. It's the last moment that we aren't truly enemies. From this moment on, we will hate each other. We will never be able to look at each other the same.

I'm done begging. And he's done talking.

He yanks me hard until I fall to my knees, and then he resumes dragging me. Once again, I try to dig my nails into his hand, but I end up just grabbing onto his wrist to keep him from ripping my hair out as he drags me.

Suddenly, he stops.

I know why.

Fear builds inside me like a windstorm. If only I had magical powers that would allow me to release the storm inside me on this room. I could destroy everything so much easier that way.

I know Beckett has to release my hair to grab my arms, my legs. So I wait patiently for my moment.

He releases.

I try to run. I scramble onto my feet and start to dive.

But he's smarter than me. He anticipates my move and kicks my feet out from under me. As I'm falling, he grabs one arm and twists it behind my back so forcefully that he's about to pop my shoulder out of its socket.

I can feel the tears welling, the pain radiating through my arm and down my spine.

"Give me your other hand," he growls.

No. I won't give in.

"Break my arm if you have to, but I won't ever submit to you."

My other hand reaches out, trying to find the chains I know he plans to tie me to. *Maybe if I grab one, I can use it as a weapon against him?*

I find a chain.

I sling it as hard as I can at Beckett's head.

I feel the weight hit him.

But he's like me. He must be used to the pain. He doesn't even react.

Instead, he once again kicks my feet out from underneath me. I reach out with the hand he isn't holding to try and catch myself from hitting the ground.

No.

I feel the cold metal clamping around my other hand.

He won.

I can keep fighting, but there is nothing I can do now. I can't break the chains holding me.

With one arm encapsulated, he grabs my arm on the floor and yanks me up. I try to kick, to fight, I even spit to try and get him to stop. He's relentless.

My free hand goes into the next handcuff over my head, and finally, my arms are locked in a wide V over my head.

I get in several vicious kicks as he slides down my body and moves to grab my ankles. But I'm weak compared to him. He attaches a chain with a metal cuff to each ankle until my legs are spread apart, and I can't move.

And then he's standing in front of me looking solemn. I know what comes next, and it's the worst. He still won't look beyond my eyes to my naked body. I stripped myself of clothes rather than have someone else strip me, but that was the only control over the situation I have.

"Please," I say, one last time.

I can hear him swallow, hear the pain in his throat, see the heartbreak on his face. But he won't stop.

We both know it.

Then I feel the gag against my mouth. I open—I'm the one making this decision, not him. He ties it tightly around the back of my head.

One more sense gone.

I can't move.

I can't talk.

I try to turn off my hearing before he places the earplugs into my ears, cutting off all sound.

I can't move.

I can't talk.

I can't hear.

There is one step left, and it's the worst of them all.

I close my eyes—trying to gain my composure before the blindfold goes around my eyes. Once it's on, I open my eyes. I can't see anything.

I can't move.

I can't talk.

I can't hear.

I can't see.

The only sense left is smell, and I'm pretty sure they'd cut that sense off too if there were another way for me to breathe.

He's taken everything from me. I no longer have any control over my body. The only thing I could do is try to cry out a safe word. That would get my gag removed long enough to see if I was using my safe word or not.

But that would only be a temporary solution. Once they removed my gag, and I didn't call out my safe word, they'd resume.

I take a deep breath through my nose, trying to gain any knowledge of who is in the room or what's going to happen next. I don't smell anything except smoke. I never got a good whiff of Beckett, so I don't know what he smells like. I'll have no idea if he's the one touching me or someone else.

Right now, no one is touching me.

The not knowing, the waiting—that's the worst part of this all.

I try to meditate in my head, but I've never been very good at meditating. I can feel my pulse rushing, my body warming, sweat bubbling on my forehead and neck.

And then it starts.

Hands...

So many hands touching my body that I can't keep track.

Being sensory deprived like this makes it impossible to tune out the touching, the feeling. It all becomes more intensified. A light brush of a hand feels like a million nerve endings bursting. A rough grasp feels like a bone breaking. A slap feels like a gale-force wind hitting my face.

I can't anticipate a touch or a slap.

I can't decipher if the feelings are enjoyable or perverted.

I can't fight back.

I'm helpless.

The one place I never thought I'd be.

Hands start invading my body. Gripping my breasts. Spreading my legs. Dipping into my pussy, my asshole.

Make it stop.

Make it all go away.

Langston. Think about Langston. Think about what you are doing to him, for him. Think about all that you've lost. Think about who you are doing this for.

18
LANGSTON

I'M DRAGGED out of the room by my arms. I don't know where I'm being taken, and I don't care. My mind is on a loop of all things Liesel.

My brain has decided for the moment that Liesel's snarky comments are my favorite thing about her, replaying her highlights.

"One touch and your cock is as hard as steel."

"One kiss and I'm all you can think about."

"This is war, killer."

I smile at the last one.

A door opens in front of me, and the men turn us sideways so we can all fit through. Then, I'm being shoved into a tub. Warm water and bath salts sting my back, but I don't even have the energy to hiss or protest.

"Stay in the water for at least a half-hour. It will help. To your left, there is a tray of food for you to eat and a remote to turn off the TV if you prefer not to watch. The next challenge starts in five minutes," one of the men says.

And then they leave.

I tilt my head up. I'm in a bathroom, soaking in a large

tub filled with bath salts that have started to soothe the ache on my back.

Why do I feel so weak? I don't remember them doing anything that should make me feel this terrible.

I inhale and get a whiff of a burger.

I turn to my left, and I find a gourmet looking burger, a milkshake, fries, a pizza, a salad, and some cake looking thing. I want it all.

I grab the milkshake first, knowing I'll be able to get those calories in with the least amount of effort. Then I can move to what my stomach is really craving: that damn burger.

I suck down the milkshake. Within seconds, my headache is gone, and my head clears.

I feel like I've been drugged, and the drugs are just starting to leave my system.

Maybe I was?

The screen in front of me starts flashing, and then I see the room I was just in. I cringe looking at it. I can't watch whoever goes next.

I see Liesel walk in, followed by Beckett, and I know I won't be able to tear my eyes away.

I watch them read the cards.

Please, just get out. I want to scream at them that it's not worth it.

Beckett's hand is on the back of her dress, and he's unzipping it.

Motherfucker.

I told him not to touch her, not to fuck her.

The next thing I know, they are both naked, and I'm terrified. *Why did they willingly get undressed?*

Why?

WHY?

Then, the monster's voice starts the challenge.

Liesel runs.

Why is she running?

Beckett chases her.

There is so much smoke initially; it makes it hard to see. My own eyes begin to water just thinking about how it feels to be in that room.

Then the smoke lessens as Beckett catches her.

She keeps fighting.

My Liesel.

I'm so sorry.

You are mine to play with. Mine to torture. Mine to kill.

You owe me penance, not him.

And yet, she'll pay the price all the same unless she mutters her safe word.

Save yourself.

Save me.

This is torture watching her suffer. It might be worse than going through it myself.

I should turn the screen off. I can't help her, and this will just hurt me. But I can't leave her alone.

We may be enemies, but she's *my* enemy—*mine*. No one else gets to touch her.

And then my heart stops. I wouldn't be shocked if I died from a stroke or heart attack watching Beckett restrain her.

My chest rages with pain; my heart thumps hard then slow, fast and quiet. It doesn't know what to do; it's just yelling at me to get my ass out of the water and go save her.

But I can't save her. Only she can save herself.

Beckett has her tied, her arms and legs spread in the center of the room.

She can handle this. She's strong.

And then I see what comes next.

A gag around her mouth.

Earplugs.

A blindfold.

She must be going crazy inside being so sensory deprived.

I'm going to lose it.

My chest pounds for her. I don't know what I feel for Liesel other than possessiveness, and anger at her fucking sins.

But this...

This is unthinkable for her to endure.

Except, she's endured it before. And she came back. *Why did she come back?*

I look at Beckett—it's obvious what he's required to do next, but he's just standing there still as a statue, unsure. *Does he touch her and endure my wrath, or does he say his safe word and leave her vulnerable?*

He looks to the door.

A moment later, three men have entered.

They look similar to the men who beat me.

Don't fucking touch her!

But of course, that's what they are there for—to ravish her. To make her feel out of control and so overwhelmed that she can't think straight.

To many other people, this might be their wildest fantasy —tied up, blindfolded, and fucked senseless by four hot men.

To Liesel, this is her greatest nightmare. I've seen her fuck. She has to be in complete control. I don't blame her. I'm much the same way, which is one of the many reasons why we'd never work together.

The men start touching her, groping her, and Beckett follows suit. He runs his hand down the curve of her waist and then grips her hip while a man penetrates her with his finger.

I can't watch.

I can't *not* watch.

I run out of the tub and go to the door. Water drips all over the tile floor, and I almost slip on my ass. I yank the door handle, already expecting the door to be locked.

I have to get to Liesel.

I have to stop this.

I pull harder, determined to get the door to budge. All I end up doing is pulling my side of the handle clean off. I throw my body against the door. I kick as hard as I can, but this isn't an ordinary door. This one is thick, most likely bulletproof.

I slink to the floor as my tears fall. I can't save her.

I hear a slapping sound, and that motivates me to get my ass off the floor and run to the screen.

Liesel's cheek is pink from where she was slapped.

Beckett steps up to her and slaps her.

I'm going to kill him.

And then I watch as a man slides his cock into my woman and I'm lost, so fucking lost.

Watching Waylon fuck her drove me mad—but this, this will change me in a way I haven't even figured out yet.

Does watching her get punished like this wipe her clean of the greatest sin she could commit?

No.

But it does weaken me, make me feel like she's suffered more than anyone. When I kill her, I'll be merciful. I'll make it painless and quick. Not torturous, like this.

This is pain.

There is only one time I've felt this much pain: when Liesel betrayed everything I thought I knew about her.

I never thought helplessly watching her put herself into a situation like this would make me feel anything for her. I thought my heart had closed to her permanently, but I was wrong.

This.

This...

It changes everything.

I have to win. I can't let her endure more than this. I don't know how many rounds are left, but if she doesn't mutter her safe word now, I have to get her to early in the next round. I have to convince her. Hopefully, this experience will remind her to not push any further.

Maybe if I promise to give her the money when I win, she'll stop?

I don't know if she'll believe me, but I have to try.

I can't fucking go through this again.

I can't.

I crumple to the floor, glued to the TV as my heart breaks more and more for the girl who used to live across the street from me. To the girl who, at one point in my life, meant everything. *Maybe she means more to me now than I'll ever admit to myself?*

Tears continue to stream down my face. I realize that Beckett's task is to repeat one of the men's actions on Liesel. When there is nothing left for Beckett to repeat but fuck her, he says his safe word.

When he turns and looks at the camera, there are tears in his swollen eyes. He hardly even knows Liesel, and he's a fucking mess.

I'm not going to survive this.

I scream my own safe word, wishing that I could make it stop, but no one is listening to me. No one will come.

I pray to God that this is fake, that this is all a show Liesel is putting on to show me how much I fucking care about her.

I know it's not, but my brain is trying anything to make sense of this.

I'm broken.

I was already broken, but this—this is as bad as it gets.

I don't know how long it goes on. I don't know when it stops, but at some point, I look at the screen, and she's no longer on it.

That's when I collapse again. I fall into the darkness of sleep, and that's where I plan on spending the rest of my life: swimming in the dark.

19

LIESEL

I'M BARELY conscious as I'm dragged out of the room, but I survived.

Now, I get a break. A hot bath and warm food. I won't be watching any of the other rounds. I don't care. I just need to refocus before my next round.

A door is opened in front of me, and I'm pushed inside.

There is a body on the floor.

"Sorry, we went to the wrong room." The men start to turn and lead me away.

"Stop. I want to stay here."

The men look at each other and shrug. Then they leave me barely able to stand on my own two feet. Langston better not have eaten all the food because I'm going to need something to eat.

As soon as the door is locked behind me, I stumble forward to Langston's body on the ground, and I collapse next to him.

I can hear him breathing. *He's alive, just passed out.*

He looks so beautifully broken lying on the floor. I reach out and stroke his hair back off his forehead. I want to press my lips to him. I want to feel him moan against my mouth after everything we've just been through—I need something warm and comforting.

He opens his eyes.

"Are you real?" he asks.

I smile. "I'm real. I survived, just like you."

"What are you doing here?"

"A room mixup, but it worked out in my favor."

He finally smiles. "Mine too."

"Think you can sit up?"

"Do you think you can?"

I sigh. "As long as you promise to feed me lots of pizza."

"That I can do."

We both inch up slowly until we are in a sitting position leaning against the base of the tub. Langston reaches back and grabs a towel and hands it to me. It's only then I remember I'm still naked.

"Thanks," I mumble as I wrap the towel around my body. He ties a towel around his waist.

Then he pulls the tray of food in front of us. I grab a slice of pizza, and he grabs the burger. We both eat, trying to regain some strength.

"You care about me," I say.

He stops mid-bite.

"No, I don't," he says.

I smile brighter. "Liar. You care about me."

He frowns and shakes his head. "I don't."

"You can't lie anymore. I know the truth."

"How?"

I grin around a bite of pizza as he stares deeply into my eyes. I can feel my cheeks blushing like a schoolgirl who just found out her crush likes her.

"You called out your safe word."

He frowns. "And that means I care about you?"

I nod. "You would have only said your safe word to get them to stop hurting me."

"Explain."

I laugh. "My challenge was to last until someone said their safe word to try and get it to stop. You were that person. You stopped my suffering Langston, which means you must have been suffering a lot watching me."

It was the same rules last time, but last time I was here, there was no one here that personally knew me. It took much longer for someone to say their safe word to try and stop my pain.

"Does that mean I'm out of the game?" Langston asks.

"No, you didn't say it as part of your challenge. You're still in. But if you want out, just say it at the beginning of the next round."

He nods.

I go back to happily scarfing down my pizza.

"I care."

His words make my heart skip a beat.

"I care about you. But I still hate you," he says.

I bite my bottom lip to hide my pleasure at hearing those words.

"Same," I say.

His eyes light up at my voice.

We both finish eating all the food on the tray.

"Get in the tub. You must be aching," Langston says.

I nod.

He turns the hot water on to warm up the tub and then holds out his hand to me. I take it, and he pulls me up into a standing position.

I let my towel fall to the floor, but this time, Langston doesn't take in my body.

"It's okay, you can look at me," I say.

He shakes his head. "If I do, I won't be able to stop. I'll

run my eyes over every inch of your body, looking for all the ways you were hurt. And you don't need to be violated again, even by me."

What happened in there broke him more than it broke me. Maybe because I'm already in a million pieces.

I step into the water and sink down, expecting Langston to join me, to wash me, something.

He doesn't.

He can barely even look at me.

"What happens next?" Langston asks with a heavy voice.

"The final round."

"And that round is worse than this one?"

I shrug. "It can be."

"When it starts, I want you to say your safe word immediately. Say it and end this. I'll give you all the money I stole back. I'll give you more than that if you want. I'll make our fight fair again, just end this."

I close my eyes. *I wish it were that simple.*

"I can't."

"Yes, you can." Langston grabs my hands, and I open my eyes to look at him. "You entered this for the money. I'll deposit the money back in your account, plus a couple of extra million. Just say your safe word."

I touch Langston's face. For a moment, he looks like the boy I used to know. Bright, warm, and a little bit mischievous, with a haunting brokenness behind his eyes.

There is a knock at the door, saving me from more conversation. A man enters holding our clothes.

"Be ready in fifteen minutes for the final round," he says, placing our clothes on the back of a chair.

We both nod at him.

"We need to get dressed," I say, getting out of the tub and drying off. I don't care if Langston is watching me or not.

We both get dressed, and I find the note with my safe word attached to the inside of my dress.

I pull it out and read it.

Unicorn.

Langston studies me. "You didn't even read your safe word until this moment, did you?"

I shake my head.

"I should have called you my wild thing instead of huntress," he says, impressed.

I smile. I like hearing him call me his anything.

"Promise me you'll use your safe word if things go too far," Langston says.

"I promise," but it's just another lie. There is only one thing that will stop me, and he's standing in front of me in a tux.

20
LANGSTON

I WANT to kill Liesel for what she did. But I'd also die to protect her.

It's confusing, but it's how I feel.

Liesel is once again in her swanky black dress. I'm in my tux. We only have minutes left until the final round begins. I don't know how many competitors we face, or if we are the only two left. We'll find out soon enough.

"How do you feel?" she asks, while she traces her hands up my forearms to my biceps, sending chills up my body.

"Better when you do that."

She smiles. "I'm serious. Did you get enough to eat? Did you soak long enough? Did—"

I lean down and kiss her. She tastes like marinara sauce mixed with lavender, which makes me grin into the kiss. Her lips are soft and warm; they respond immediately to my touch. I'm the only man who gets to kiss her. That may be how it should be, but it's not reality. I hate that this can't be our reality.

My tongue pushes into her mouth, and she jerks back. But as my tongue massages her bottom lip, she lets me into her mouth. The attack of her tongue against mine proves that this is what our mouths were always meant to be doing —kissing each other.

I can feel the minutes and seconds ticking by; we don't have forever. Our time together is precious. Soon, there will be a knock on the door, and this kiss will be nothing but a memory.

But I hope it's a memory I'll be able to take with me long after. In the middle of the challenges we are about to face, I hope this brings us peace.

"Thank you," she says as my lips leave hers.

"Don't ever thank me for kissing you. Kissing you is a gift to me as much as it is for you."

I tuck a strand of her hair behind her ear. "No wig tonight?"

She shakes her head. "Beckett pulled it off in the last round; everyone knows I have blonde hair. So tonight, I'm going in as me."

"Whatever you say, Ms. White."

She blushes, and her eyes sparkle.

"Turn around."

She does, and I help her fasten her mask to her face. My fingers brush against her bare arms when I'm done, and I watch her goosebumps rise. A small part of me is excited about what this round could entail. It could finally give me a reason to fuck Liesel.

I don't want this twisted game to be the reason that I sink my cock into her. But my cock is excited all the same.

"Turn around," Liesel says, repeating my words.

I do, and she stands on her tiptoes to reach my head where she can fasten my mask.

There is a knock at the door just as she finishes.

Instinctively, I step in front of her, and my hand reaches back to hold hers, to protect her.

"If you'll follow me this way, we are about to start the final round," the man says and then starts walking.

I don't let go of Liesel's hand as we start following the man out of the room. The man leads us down the hallway to the same room we both faced our previous challenge.

I stop and turn to Liesel before we enter.

"I will do everything I can to protect you. I can't fail—not again."

She releases my hand. "I can't let you protect me," she whispers.

Then she walks past me and into the room like she's the CEO entering a boardroom—full of sass and determination.

I walk in behind her with her words ringing in my ear. *She won't let me protect her.*

Well, too fucking bad. After the life we've both lived, she deserves my protection. I'm the only one who gets to kill her.

To my shock, we are the only two in the room. I glance to Liesel, who looks just as stunned. *Are we the only two who made it to the final round?*

The voice appears. "Welcome to the final round. Only two contestants remain. Each of you have cards lying on the table. The final round begins in five minutes."

Liesel and I both walk over to the table with the cards.

We pick up our respective cards in unison.

I'm dying to know what's on her card, but I doubt that's allowed.

So instead, I focus on reading mine:

A woman you know will be tied to a bed. Fuck her so that your competitor thinks you're hurting her. You will have thirty minutes to strike fear into your competitor. You will then receive new instructions. If your competitor shows no fear, you've failed.

. . .

I just have to make Liesel think I'm hurting this woman, not actually inflict pain. I don't know who the woman is, but it doesn't seem so terrible. Although, Liesel will hate me more than she already does.

Liesel finishes reading her card. She doesn't show any emotion. I don't know what her card says, but I'm guessing something similar to mine.

Just please don't let it involve her being tied up again. I won't be able to sit by and watch that happen.

Smoke starts billowing into the room, the indication that the game is about to start.

"Your thirty minutes start now," the wicked voice says.

Liesel and I exchange glances through the evaporating smoke. Apparently, the smoke won't be hanging around this time.

Two beds appear side by side in front of us.

"Phoenix?" I ask, looking to the woman tied to the bed right in front of me. *It can't be. Did they kidnap her?* She would never agree to be here.

"Waylon," Liesel whispers.

My eyes cut from Phoenix tied to the first bed to Waylon tied to the other.

What the hell is going on?

I look to Liesel, like she might have an explanation for this. If this happened last time, she could have at least warned me.

Liesel isn't looking at me; she's walking toward Waylon's bed. His arms and legs are tied in an X to the bedposts, same as Phoenix.

I run to Phoenix's side.

"It's okay," she whispers. "I agreed."

My heart clenches. I don't know if she understands what

she agreed to or not, but her words at least comfort me. Now isn't the time to ask questions, though.

I look deep into Phoenix's eyes, letting her know what is about to happen as best as I can with just one look.

Phoenix and I aren't as good at understanding each other with looks as Liesel and I are, but it's pretty clear what I'm asking in this situation.

"Yes," she whispers, her voice aching.

My eyes cut over to Liesel, who is already undressing Waylon. Her lips are pressed to his, just as they were to mine a few moments ago.

My stomach twists, wishing it were me tied to her bed.

Liesel doesn't look over at me. She just keeps kissing and moaning.

Jesus, I can't focus on that.

But how am I going to strike fear in her if she won't even look at me? If she looks at me, she'll know I'm just doing whatever is on my card. She won't be any more afraid of me than she already is.

Phoenix is tied to the bed loosely with rope—rope I can easily pull off. I can fuck her in any position in any place in this room.

My mind races, thinking about what I can do to scare Liesel.

I remove my jacket and then roll my sleeves up.

"Lang—" Phoenix starts, but I throw my hand over her mouth, silencing her.

She takes the hint and doesn't speak when I remove my hand.

Liesel and Waylon, on the other hand, are a non-stop moan-fest. All I hear is moaning and groaning coming from their direction.

I try to shut them out, but that's impossible. My fists clench, and my body fills with adrenaline and rage. I actually think it's going to be easier than I thought to get Liesel to fear me.

I growl. It's loud, demanding the attention of everyone in the room as I grab the ropes at Phoenix's ankles and rip them hard. The ropes break free from the posts at the end of the bed.

Phoenix gasps, but she's used to my loud, controlling behavior. I can be as rough as I want, and it won't bother her. She'll welcome it.

Phoenix is wearing black leggings and a long-sleeved black shirt. She has a black mask over her eyes. Strangely, the mask only adds to Phoenix's outfit—like she should always be wearing a mask.

Even though I've fucked Phoenix plenty of times, it feels strange, almost immoral to do it now.

She chose you. She came to you. She wants you.

I glance over at Liesel on top of Waylon. She hasn't removed any of her clothes, but I know his cock is about to slide between her legs.

Focus on Phoenix, on fucking her.

But what if she isn't the one I crave anymore?

I grab Phoenix's legs with all my rage and flip her over until the rope at her arms twists, tightening the bindings.

She gasps at the sudden movement, at her body twisting in an uncomfortable way. But that's what this is about—fucking her so forcefully and so painfully that Liesel is terrified of me.

I climb onto the bed and rip her leggings back until her ass is showing. I slap her ass red.

She grunts, but when I reach between her legs, I feel how wet she is.

She likes it.

She would be the perfect match for me, unlike Liesel,

who would be horrified if I touched her like this—untamed and wild.

I unzip my pants, pull myself out, and roughly enter her from behind. My hand reaches out to grab her face and shove my fingers into her mouth, pulling on her cheek. Her saliva drips down her chin as I pound into her.

Don't look at Liesel.

Focus on fucking Phoenix. Focus on making it blissful for Phoenix; that's the best way to frighten Liesel. If she sees Phoenix loving how rough I am, Liesel will be mortified.

I have no doubt what the next challenge is—fucking Liesel. I'm not sure I can handle it. Not after she just fucked Waylon. Not after I just fucked Phoenix. *Not like this.*

I want to win.

I want to protect Liesel.

How do I do that?

The bed creaks and breaks beneath us; that's how hard I've been fucking Phoenix. In such a trance that I didn't notice her sobs, her tears, her pain.

Phoenix likes the pain, though. I didn't break her.

One glance over at the single tear floating in Liesel's eye tells me I broke her.

21
LIESEL

This is all a game.

A twisted.

Fucked up.

Evil game.

Langston may not realize how dangerous this game is yet, but he will soon.

I ride Waylon's cock like I have an unhealthy level of love for him. My body pumps over his harder and faster; my eyes are wild with love and lust. I even let my eyes water a little. I haven't cried in years, but this—seeing Langston next to me, pretending to hurt his wife while I pretend that fucking Waylon is my favorite thing in the world, makes me insane.

It pushes me to the edge of spilling my heart. To telling every rotten truth. To stop the lies between Langston and me. But if I did, we'd both be destroyed.

So I keep pretending. I like Waylon—truly, I do, but I don't love him. I'm incapable of love.

Yet, by the way that Langston keeps shooting me dirty glances, it's clear he believes I love the man whose cock is inside me.

Mission accomplished.

That was what I was supposed to do according to my card. Make Langston think I'm in love with Waylon. And I'm sure Langston's told him to make me afraid of him.

I don't really fear Langston any more than I did before we started, but still, I wince at every slap.

Maybe I'm lying to myself? Maybe I do fear Langston?

No, I'm just afraid of what will come next. I can't be with Langston in that way...

Waylon moans, and I turn my attention back to him. I feel him close to coming. I rock my hips against him, pushing him closer to orgasm.

"Come with me, baby," he says.

I smile at him and stroke his hair like his words are melting my heart.

I nod. "Together."

Then I feel his warm cum inside me at the same time I yell out his name—faking an orgasm, something I've perfected over the years.

Once he's done shooting cum into my body, I lean forward and kiss him tenderly on the lips.

"Thank you," I whisper.

"My pleasure. I love fucking you here where everyone is watching, knowing that you can have another man's cock in you, but that you belong to me, no one else."

"Yours," I whisper against his lips.

I feel Langston's hot stare on me. I hear his growl and the rough slapping of skin as he fucks Phoenix with everything he has. Every noise bites into me.

He's taking out his frustration with me on Phoenix. And instead of feeling pity for the woman, I feel jealousy. I wish I were the one Langston was fucking that hard.

But my body and mind couldn't handle it. Langston is

too much for me. Maybe that's why I chose Waylon—he's safe.

I continue to kiss Waylon sweetly until our time is up. I've already completed my mission, and I'm just trying to focus on anything else except Langston going to town on Phoenix.

The slapping.

The kissing.

The grunting.

The moaning.

The smell of hot sex.

It's impossible to shut out.

I sigh into Waylon's lips.

"I love you, baby," he says.

I kiss him. I never say the words back because our time is up.

"You both passed the first round. You have five minutes to collect yourself before we proceed," the voice says.

I take off. I need out of the room. I need to breathe without smelling Langston. Need to think without Langston popping into my mind. Touch without Langston's lips branding into my memory as he kisses me.

I want to run to the top deck to get some air, but Langston will find me there, and I need some space away from him to make sure I know what I'm doing.

I dart into one of the bathrooms and lock the door behind me.

I take deep, hard breaths, filling my lungs with warm oxygen as I grab onto the sink and look at myself in the mirror.

I'm doing the right thing.

I'm going to win.

I have to win.

22
LANGSTON

I REALLY DO HATE LIESEL.

And yet, I've never wanted her more.

As frustrating as that was, it was also the most erotic moment of my life.

I've spent my entire life needing to fuck Liesel and yet not having her. That was the closest we've ever gotten, and it was nowhere near enough.

Hearing her, smelling her, seeing her, but not being able to touch her, that was my own special kind of hell. One I hope to rectify soon.

Five minutes.

That's how long we have to the next round. I watch Liesel dart out of the room. Immediately, I sprint after her, leaving Phoenix still tied to the bed.

Of all the ways I've imagined Liesel and me fucking for the first time, this isn't what I'd choose. Minutes after we were both forced to fuck other people in the same room while being watched by strangers isn't exactly ideal.

Five minutes isn't long enough either, but at least it would be our choice.

I chase Liesel down the hallway.

She slams a door shut.

I run after her.

My pants are still undone as I chase her.

I grab the doorknob and turn, but it doesn't open.

She locked it.

"Huntress?" I ask through the door.

I wait for her to answer.

She doesn't.

I press my hand against the door as I feel the seconds ticking by. Our time to choose is ending.

If we both want to continue the game, we'll end up fucking each other. It's what I want, what I need, but I didn't want it this way.

But nothing between Liesel and me is ever what I want.

Five minutes tick by before Liesel opens the door.

She's not surprised I'm standing here. She knew.

She knew I was here. She knew and chose to keep the door shut.

Her eyes are full of apology.

I nod.

"Ready?" I ask.

"Are you?"

I have no fucking idea. The woman I've wanted all my life is about to agree to fuck me in a wicked game. I have no idea how to feel about that.

A soft smile spreads on her lips as she reads my thoughts.

"Me too," she says, and then she walks past me. Her hips sway extra hard, like she's trying to seduce me.

Although, she's had me under her spell since I was thirteen. She doesn't need to try to get me to fuck her. All she has to do is say yes.

I walk down the hallway, redoing my pants even though I

know they are probably going to be ripped from my body soon.

What will it feel like to fuck Liesel? Like a fucking atomic bomb going off.

Liesel walks back into the room two seconds before I do. The setup is the same, but now Phoenix and Waylon are gone. I should be worried about Phoenix, but I'm not. She told me she came here voluntarily, and she can take care of herself. Plus, I don't want to think of anything else while I'm with Liesel.

"Read your cards, and the game starts in five minutes," the voice says.

We see the cards with our names on it once again on the table, and exchange glances at each other. After this moment, everything is going to change.

I pick up my card reluctantly and flip it over.

Fuck her like you've always wanted to. Take no mercy. Make her hate you. Make her fear you. Make her say her safe word.

I suck in a long breath. Somehow, I knew what was on the card. I knew the card would make her hate me if I were to succeed. The one positive is that Liesel already hates me, so that part wouldn't change if I complete my challenge.

I don't know if I'm going to be able to fuck in her a way that makes her say her safe word, though. She's been through a lot, me taking her control away and fucking her hard wouldn't force her to quit.

Fuck her like you've always wanted to.

That was the first order. So first, I can fuck her how I've always wanted to—a loophole.

First, fuck her like I want to.

Then, fuck her to make her fear me, to get her to say her safe word.

I'll worry about the second part later, but I've been dreaming about the first task since I hit puberty.

Liesel doesn't look at me. She's still staring at her card; her lips are moving along with the words. I've never wished more that I could read lips.

Look at me, huntress.

She doesn't.

She drops her card and stares at it on the ground as our time ticks down.

"You may begin. You have as long as it takes until one of you says your safe word," the voice says.

I take a step toward Liesel, and she takes a step back.

I frown.

She's already afraid of me.

That or her card...?

I take another step. She takes another step back.

"I'm not going to hurt you."

"Yes, you will, killer."

Her words sting, but they are also the truth. I'm always hurting her. *Why would she think this would be any different?*

I take another step, and she trembles.

I may have done too well in the previous round if she's this afraid of me.

"Huntress, I won't hurt you." *I won't do anything you don't want me to do. Someday, I'll have to kill you, but that day isn't today.*

Another step, and I have her boxed into a corner. There is nowhere for her to go.

"Trust me," I whisper.

I reach out my hand slowly to touch her, and she cringes away.

It crushes me.

So instead, I grab her wrist and place it against my heart.

"I'm scared too."

She swallows her pain, trying to lock it inside. Really, I want her to unleash it on me. I deserve to feel her pain as much as I need to feel her pleasure. I've fucked up as much as she has. I deserve to die just like she does.

She closes her eyes, keeping her hand on my heart.

I let her hold her hand there for as long as it takes. This challenge can last as long as we need. I'm not going to rush our first time. I'm going to let every moment linger. I'm going to memorize every little thing because I don't know if I'll ever get this chance again.

I close my eyes too—just feeling her warm hand through my shirt.

My heart aches for more, but also for this moment to last forever.

Once I feel that Liesel is ready for more, I reach my hands out and grab her face, lifting it gently toward mine. I open my eyes, watching her reaction as my lips hover over hers.

I want this kiss more than I want to breathe. And my body craves what comes next more than anything else. I'd trade life itself for a chance with her.

Her eyes open, and for a moment, it feels like old times. We share a direct connection between our hearts, souls, and minds.

I win, her eyes say.

I frown, not understanding.

What did her card say?

It doesn't matter. She can win the game for all I care; I just want her. That's me winning.

I lean closer, closing the gap until my lips all but brush against hers.

"Unicorn," she whispers.

I raise an eyebrow in confusion.

"That concludes the game. Mr. Pearce is the winner," the voice says.

I stare at Liesel, but she's no longer looking at me.

I grab her chin, trying to force her to look at me. I don't understand how she could go through what she did and yet couldn't endure a simple kiss from me.

Her face has morphed, and she is no longer open to me. I can't see what she's thinking or feeling.

Two men enter, grab onto Liesel's arms, and lead her out of the room.

Suddenly, I'm alone.

I won.

I don't give a shit about the money.

"I'll escort you to meet the owners, Mr. Pearce. There you will be able to collect the twenty million dollar prize," Mr. Reyes says.

I nod. "Lead the way."

23
LIESEL

It's over.

I take a deep breath, unsure of my actions.

It had to be done. I didn't have a choice.

But I know how this ends.

That makes me smile, even though he's going to hate me even worse than he already does.

The men continue to hold onto my arms as they lead me out of the room and up to the top deck. There is a small dingy boat waiting to take me to shore. They lead me to it and release my arms once I'm inside the small raft-like boat.

"Thank you for playing, Ms. White. You'll be taken back to shore now," one of the men says.

I nod.

They continue to stand there until the raft is lowered into the water, and there is no way for me to escape and climb back on board.

"I'm Kyo. We should be back to shore in the next twenty minutes," he says.

"Thank you, Kyo."

He starts the engine once we've hit the water, and we pull away.

I did the right thing.

I did the right thing.

I did the right thing.

Those words continue to play over and over in my head the entire twenty minutes the dingy takes us to shore.

I did the right thing.

I did the right thing.

I did the right thing.

I can't look back at the yacht. I can't look back, hoping to find Langston. What's done is done.

I did the right thing.

I had no other choice.

I already know how this ends. He'll be fine.

The dingy stops back at the dock, and Kyo helps me off.

"Your ride will be here shortly. Can I get you anything else?" Kyo says when we are both standing on the dock.

I shake my head and then walk down the dock to where Maxwell is standing outside of a limo.

"Did you win?" he asks.

"Yea. Yea, I did."

He smiles. "Good. Now don't give me a heart attack like that again."

I smile back.

He helps me into the back of the limo, before heading to the front to drive me.

I lean my head against the headrest and close my eyes, trying to forget everything.

I should be happy. If I'm lucky, I'll have a few days of freedom.

A child's squeal jolts my eyes open.

I stare out the window and see two kids playing together

with a ball in a nearby park. Phoenix is standing nearby, watching them with a smile on her face.

Kids.

Two beautiful, healthy kids.

Langston wasn't lying. He's a father. These are his kids.

I fucked up.

I did the wrong thing.

24
LANGSTON

"THIS WAY," Mr. Reyes says.

I follow Mr. Reyes out of the game room and down a hallway. He leads me through the ship to a thick, sealed door that has all of the highest tech—facial recognition, thumb scanner, and multiple external-facing cameras.

The door unlocks, and Mr. Reyes holds it open for me. I step inside cautiously, knowing a trap when I see one.

The door locks behind me. I don't even jump. I knew it was going to happen, and I accept it. I want to meet the owner of this operation. I want to look him in the face and demand answers for what he did to Liesel. I know she didn't do this willingly the first time. I'm not even sure she did this willingly the second time.

I wish I had a gun, a weapon. I always feel less anxious with a gun on me. But I'm thankful that at least Liesel is off the ship. I don't feel her presence anymore.

The coward I'm about to meet had to ensure that I met him in this room, the only room on the yacht strong enough to hold me. He knew the only way to get me here was if I won, if I saw all the darkness that he forced Liesel to endure

—that alone would motivate me to meet the man behind the voice, behind the darkness.

He's not the devil. The devil is cunning; he has a plan. This man is just a vile pansy who will spend his life rotting in hell.

"Congratulations on your win, Mr. Pearce," the man says. He's sitting in a chair in the shadows, so I can't see his face.

But I can finally hear his voice unmodified, and I recognize it.

"Show your face, you coward."

"Why? I'm sure by now you've figured out who I am."

"I have. I want to look you in the eyes when I kill you."

He laughs.

I scan the room. It seems like it's just the two of us, but this man must have set the trap ages ago. He will have everything planned. I have to be careful and find the perfect timing.

"What do you want with me? Why set up this elaborate game?"

"You claim Liesel belongs to you, but she's always belonged to me. Always."

"And how did this game prove that?"

"We've been playing these games for years. She's always required to win, always required to do as I say. This is the first time I told her to lose."

"Why?" This isn't just about Liesel. This is about so much more. It's about that damn letter Liesel and I accidentally split in half when we were eighteen. This man seeks the treasure—he might have known about it from the moment he met Liesel. He might have been playing her all along.

But does he control her?

Or is she playing him like she so often plays me?

That's a question for Liesel. This bastard needs to die.

"I guess I'll just have to kill you without seeing the whites of your eyes. It makes no difference to me." I goad him, giving him one last chance to step forward.

He doesn't take the bait.

"I won't be the one dying tonight," he says.

I make my move.

I dart forward into the shadows, not sure what I'm going to find. He could be holding a gun aimed at my head for all I know, but I've faced worse. Liesel lost on purpose, so I would end up here. I've failed Liesel too many times; I won't disappoint her again.

I go for his head, grabbing him by the neck. I squeeze and hold on with everything I have, tackling him to the ground and out of the shadows.

Waylon Brown.

The fucking bastard.

There is so much I don't understand, but what I do know is that he's a sick fucker who hurt Liesel and is using her to get the treasure.

I punch him in the eye before I feel a bullet hit my back.

A second bullet.

A third.

It doesn't stop me from trying to strangle Waylon.

Now, it's just a matter of time.

Will I lose consciousness and bleed to death, or will Waylon stop breathing first?

His face is red.

My body is strong.

I can kill him before I'm taken down.

I can.

I must...

25
LIESEL

"STOP THE CAR!" I yell.

The limo continues moving forward. I don't think Maxwell can hear me, and I'm not going to wait to figure out how to find the button that connects me to the front of the limo.

I open my door and roll out, hitting the pavement hard in my dress and heels. I scramble to my feet quickly and start to run in Phoenix's direction. I need to get to her before she realizes who's coming for her. If she recognizes me, she'll run away before I get a chance to talk to her.

Luckily, she's facing the kids playing in the park. I can't see the kids easily, but it's not them I need to convince. Although, I'd love to get a closer look at the two young kids —bask in the traits that are Langston.

I don't have time for that.

When I'm almost to Phoenix, I speak.

"It was a trap," I say, not sure how many words I'll be able to get out and choosing the most important ones first.

She turns and looks at me with wide eyes and a puzzled expression.

I huff and grab her arms, hoping I'm stronger than her or the skills Langston taught me as a kid will be good enough to force her to listen to me. The only problem is Langston has probably taught her the same tricks.

"Get off of me," she tries to shake me off her arm, but I don't let go.

"Listen to me. I'm trying to help you."

"Help? You don't know the meaning of the word. Langston will be here soon, and he'll kidnap you and drag you back to the island. Or better yet, kill you."

"No, he won't. I set him up. It was a trap. He might escape, but it won't be anytime soon, and while he's gone..." I nod in the direction of the kids.

"The kids are in danger," Phoenix finishes my sentence with a gasp.

"Go, get them out of here. Somewhere safe," I say.

She turns, and I think she's heard me and is going to go protect her kids when she suddenly turns back. Her hand flies up, slapping me hard across the cheek.

I feel the sting all the way through my body. I deserve it. I deserve so much more. I didn't believe the kids were real. I thought it was all a lie. But now I know, and I would never put children in danger for my own benefit.

I don't know if it would have changed what I did. I had to do it, but I would have ensured the kids were safe, that Phoenix was safe.

Phoenix gives me a smug smirk, and then she runs toward her kids, yelling at them to get in their car.

Satisfied that Phoenix will keep the kids safe, I run back to the limo. Maxwell is now out of the limo and walking toward me.

"What the hell? You could have been seriously hurt," he says.

"Drive me to Teterboro airport," I say, marching to the car.

"What happened?"

"It doesn't matter. Just drive me to the airport."

He shakes his head. "Not until you tell me what's going on. My job is to protect you; I can't do that if I don't know what's happening."

I don't trust him. There is no way I'm telling him anything. "This isn't negotiable, Max. Give me your cell phone, then get in the car and drive."

I hold out my hand, and Maxwell eventually tosses his phone to me before I stomp to the back door, open it, and climb in.

I watch from the window as Max curses and then eventually returns to the driver's seat and starts to drive.

I call Enzo.

No answer.

I leave a message saying Langston is in trouble.

I call Kai.

No answer.

I leave a message saying Langston is in trouble.

I call Zeke.

No answer.

I leave a message saying Langston is in trouble.

I call Beckett.

No answer.

I leave a message saying Langston is in trouble.

That leaves...Siren.

I hate her. She betrayed me. But right now, I need her to be there for Langston above everything else.

I call Siren.

No answer.

I leave a message saying Langston is in trouble.

"Shit," I curse as we drive toward the airport.

I don't know who else to call for help.

A second later, Maxwell's phone starts ringing in my hand.

"Hello?" I say.

"Liesel, what's going on?" Siren's voice replies.

"Langston is in trouble. I fucked up. He won the game, but it was a trap." I don't include the fact that I set the trap in the first place.

"Fuck," Siren says.

There's a pause. "I'll make sure Kai and Enzo know. They'll put together an extraction team to get Langston out of there."

I sigh, relaxing. "Thank you."

"Where are you now?"

"I was headed to the airport to come persuade you guys to get your asses here to save Langston."

I can feel her smile through the phone. "Head to your apartment. Zeke and I will head to you. You need to be protected."

"I have…" I'm about to say Maxwell, but he's not really protection. Not like Zeke and Siren would be. "Thank you," is all I end up saying.

I find the button that connects me to the front of the limo. "Maxwell, take me to my apartment."

He sighs. "Will do."

And then I'm alone in uncomfortable silence. The ride to my apartment takes over an hour. I assume Zeke and Siren are back in Miami, and will take a while to get to me, but I'm not sure.

Maxwell goes up in the elevator with me, and when I get to my apartment door, he asks if I want him to come in with me.

"No, I'm exhausted. I just need to get some rest."

"Of course."

"Goodnight."

"Goodnight."

And then I open the door and walk inside. I flip the lights on. Nothing seems out of place.

My feet wobble as I walk. I need rest. This weekend was too much.

I head toward my bedroom, planning on just collapsing into bed with Max's phone, hoping that Siren calls soon to let me know they got Langston.

I flip on the lights.

And scream.

Waylon is lifeless on my bed, covered in blood.

26
LANGSTON

I YANK on the chains that have held me for the past twenty-four hours. The yacht has long ago stopped moving; I don't know where though.

I allowed myself to be tied up. I took that as the only option when I was bleeding out and too weak to fight.

But the bandages have stopped the blood from flowing, and my body has regenerated plenty of new red blood cells. These chains won't hold me much longer.

I test their strength once more. The chains are solid—only a person of abnormal strength might be able to break them. Unfortunately, I don't have that strength.

I stare at the locks around my wrists. I smile. I do, however, have the ability to pick any lock.

I glance around for something I can use to pick the lock. I don't have much to work with—the clothes on my back, a fork, a plate, and a coke can on the floor that they left me to eat.

I pick up the can and fork. *This will work.*

Five minutes later, I've carved the aluminum of the can into a lockpick.

A moment later, the locks release on my wrists, then my ankles. I'm free.

I'm being kept in a small dark room at the base of the ship. The door looks bulletproof, but when I try the handle, it's already unlocked.

Strange.

I look for something I can use as a weapon as I move up the floors of the yacht. When I make it to the kitchen, I find a drawer of knives. I put several into my pockets and then grip the largest and hold it out in front of me as I continue to creep around the ship.

After making it to the top deck, I haven't run into a single person. *Why are there no people? What the hell happened?*

"Looking for a ride?" Enzo says suddenly from above me.

I smile brightly as I shield my eyes from the sun and look up at him. A helicopter has landed on the upper deck—my escape.

"I assume you are the reason no one is on board?"

He shrugs. "We might have had something to do with it."

"But you couldn't free me?"

He sighs. "We were working on it, but we thought your prideful ass would want to save yourself."

I chuckle as I climb up the stairs to where he stands. "That's code for you couldn't get through the door."

He growls. "We were working on it."

I pat him on the shoulder. "It's good to see you. Let's get the hell out of here."

Once in the air, Enzo tends to my wounds.

"There are no bullet fragments inside. It looks like they were shooting you with rubber bullets. They left some serious marks, but nothing as bad as it could have been."

I put on the clean black shirt Enzo hands me. "Rubber bullets? Why would they do that?"

He shrugs.

"Where is everyone?" I ask.

"Phoenix and the kids are in a safe house. Kai is giving orders back home. And Zeke and Siren are protecting Liesel."

Liesel.

"Where do you want to go?"

I should say to Phoenix, to check that she and the kids are alright.

"Liesel."

He nods.

I stare out the window of the helicopter. I have so many fucking questions for Liesel, but all I want to know is the answer to one.

Did she refuse to fuck me because she didn't want to? Because she was afraid of me?

Or did she refuse because Waylon required her to lose the game?

We fly out further into the ocean instead of closer to land. I turn to Enzo.

"Where are we going?"

"They are on a smaller yacht a few miles from here. Zeke and Siren said something about it being safer than at Liesel's place. I don't know, it wasn't my decision. We won't be able to land the helicopter on it, though."

"That's okay. You can just lower me down."

He nods.

I see the small yacht floating in the distance. It's not one of the boats I recognize from Enzo and Kai's fleet. My guess is it doesn't have all the safety features that one of our regular yachts have.

So why would they bring Liesel here to keep her safe?

I find a rope in one of the storage compartments and tie it around a bolted hook then hand the rest to Enzo.

With a slight nod of our heads, he's lowering me down while I hold onto the rope. It takes a few jerky moments for Enzo to figure out the speed to lower me, but soon I'm close enough to let go and land on the upper deck of the boat.

"Siren? Liesel? Zeke?" I shout as I look around. I should have armed myself with more than a pocket of knives before I got here, but I don't think any enemies are on-board.

I head below deck and round a corner and then freeze. My eyes blink rapidly, not sure I believe the sight in front of me.

Zeke is tied up sitting in a corner, so tightly bound he can't move a muscle.

But that isn't what has me worried.

Siren is also tied up. And with tears streaming down her face, Liesel is pointing a gun at Siren's head.

I put my hands up slowly as I approach, not entirely sure what I'm walking into.

"Huntress, talk to me. What's going on?" I ask, my voice soft, soothing, and trusting.

She sobs, louder.

"If Waylon is forcing you to do this, you should know he's dead. He can't hurt you anymore."

"I know." She sobs more.

I gaze dumbly from her to Siren. I try to reassure Siren with my eyes, but Siren will barely even look at me, she's so disappointed in me.

"I think it's your turn to tell a truth about the letter, killer. Tell me something."

"Okay, I'll tell you whatever you want. Just don't hurt Siren."

"Tell me," her voice shakes. This is about more than that

stupid letter we ripped in half all those years ago, but I'll appease her if it will calm her down.

I think through all the secrets I could tell, but the one I choose is obvious. She'll figure it out soon enough if she hasn't already.

"When your father dies, the secret will be told. Others will start looking for the treasure. You will have a choice—do nothing and let them take it, or go after it and protect it."

"My father died a month ago."

I nod, already knowing that. But I wasn't sure if she did.

"So all these attacks have been people coming after the treasure?" she asks.

I nod again.

"You thought Waylon was coming after the treasure? That's why you killed him?" She's sobbing again.

"I killed him because he was hurting you."

She shakes her head. "You don't understand. Waylon would never hurt me."

"You didn't love him, Liesel. You can do so much better than that guy. He was using you."

"You don't understand. How could you? Waylon was *everything* to me."

Her words stun me. *How could she care about Waylon?*

"You killed the one person I needed in my life, so I'm going to do the same to you."

"Liesel," my voice is a warning. I start surveying my options. I don't have a gun, but I have a knife in my back pocket. That's my only option to stop her.

"I thought about killing Phoenix, but then I remembered you don't love Phoenix. You love Siren."

"If you do anything to stop her, I'll kill you," Maxwell says from beside me a second before I grab my knife. My eyes cut to him in surprise, and I see the gun he has pointed at me.

Liesel had help, that's how she was able to pull this off.

I have to reason with her. That's all I can do.

"I'll tell you everything. Everything on my half of the letter. I'll trade your life for Siren's, just don't kill her. I'll do anything," I say.

More tears stream down her face as she looks at me.

"Huntress, please."

"You've always said I was the huntress who could never kill. You're the killer; I'm the huntress. Today, the huntress becomes the killer."

Then I watch in horror as she pulls the trigger.

Thank you so much for reading Desperate Lies! Langston & Liesel's story continues in FATED LIES!

She pulled the trigger. This is war. A battle that ends with only one of us keeping our hearts...

One-click FATED LIES now >

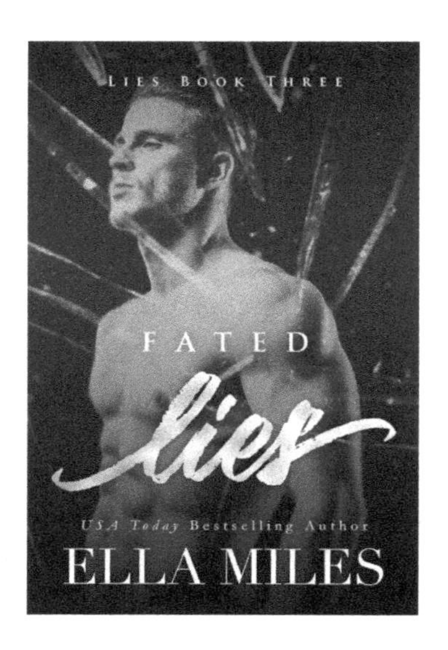

"AMAZING! Talk about edge of your seat suspenseful, non-put-down-able, emotional and gut wrenching book. WOW, just WOW!" —Reviewer

Haven't read **Enzo and Kai's story** yet?
I should have run away, found a new life, and started over.
Instead, I returned.
To find the man who sold me.
One-click Taken by Lies for FREE >

Haven't read **Zeke and Siren's story** yet?
She saved me. And now, seeing her about to be sold to the highest bidder, it's my turn to save her.
One-click Sinful Truth for FREE >

JOIN ELLA'S NEWSLETTER & NEVER MISS A SALE OR NEW RELEASE → ellamiles.com/freebooks

Love swag boxes & signed books?
SHOP MY STORE → store.ellamiles.com

ALSO BY ELLA MILES

LIES SERIES:

Lies We Share: A Prologue

Vicious Lies

Desperate Lies

Fated Lies

Cruel Lies

Dangerous Lies

Endless Lies

SINFUL TRUTHS:

Sinful Truth #1

Twisted Vow #2

Reckless Fall #3

Tangled Promise #4

Fallen Love #5

Broken Anchor #6

TRUTH OR LIES:

Taken by Lies #1

Betrayed by Truths #2

Trapped by Lies #3

Stolen by Truths #4

Possessed by Lies #5

Consumed by Truths #6

DIRTY SERIES:

Dirty Obsession

Dirty Addiction

Dirty Revenge

Dirty: The Complete Series

ALIGNED SERIES:

Aligned: Volume 1 (Free Series Starter)

Aligned: Volume 2

Aligned: Volume 3

Aligned: Volume 4

Aligned: The Complete Series Boxset

UNFORGIVABLE SERIES:

Heart of a Thief

Heart of a Liar

Heart of a Prick

Unforgivable: The Complete Series Boxset

MAYBE, DEFINITELY SERIES:

Maybe Yes

Maybe Never

Maybe Always

Definitely Yes

Definitely No

Definitely Forever

STANDALONES:

Pretend I'm Yours

Pretend We're Over

Finding Perfect

Savage Love

Too Much

Not Sorry

Hate Me or Love Me: An Enemies to Lovers Romance Collection

ABOUT THE AUTHOR

Ella Miles writes steamy romance, including everything from dark suspense romance that will leave you on the edge of your seat to contemporary romance that will leave you laughing out loud or crying. Most importantly, she wants you to feel everything her characters feel as you read.

Ella is currently living her own happily ever after near the Rocky Mountains with her high school sweetheart husband. Her heart is also taken by her goofy five year old black lab who is scared of everything, including her own shadow.

Ella is a USA Today Bestselling Author & Top 50 Bestselling Author.

Stalk Ella at:
www.ellamiles.com
ella@ellamiles.com

CPSIA information can be obtained
at www.ICGtesting.com
Printed in the USA
LVHW090409131120
671372LV00002B/193

9 781951 114756